REFUGE RESCUERS

MICHAEL ALLEN GEORGE

Brilliant Books Literary
137 Forest Park Lane Thomasville
North Carolina 27360 USA

For Tammy and Laura

It doesn't matter how things are
Or how you feel
I still often think of you

Books by Michael George

The Refuge Mystery Series

Why A Refuge	Book One
Bridge To No Good	Book Two
Grass Was Greener	Book Three
To Save The Refuge	Book Four
Without Refuge	Book five
Refuge Of Another Kind	Book Six
Places Of Refuge	Book Seven
Refuge Life And Home	Book Eight
Refuge Rescuers	Book Nine

Other Books By Michael George

Horses Lemons And Pretty Girls
More Horses And Pretty Girls
Finding Peri Gray
Of Rain Barrels And Bridges

Books Written With Bud George
And David George

Stories From Three Brothers
More Stories From Three Brothers

Books written as Michael Allen George

Why A Refuge
Places Of Refuge
Refuge Life And Home
Refuge Rescuers
More Stories From Three Brothers

Prologue

They felt like real men when they started out, but now that they were walking the third meadow, they didn't feel quite so macho. All five of them were hurting from the, for them, uncommon exercise. They simply were not used to this much physical activity. They all knew that at the end of this meadow, it was time to call a halt to this part of the hunt.

"The things we do for the company," complained one of the two lawyers in the group. "I know we're supposed to show how much we love the guns we are here to sell, but hunting one meadow would have been sufficient. If it wasn't for the fact that I actually do love shooting, this might have been too much."

"Maybe," answered the leader of the group. "but when you're involved in a multimillion dollar deal like we are, you do whatever it takes to get it done. That includes loving that bright, shiny, new shotgun in your hands."

"I know. And it's even more important to show our love for the assault rifles we'll be using next. They'll be making up the largest part of our sale."

"That's right. We go after deer next. I expect every damn one of you to shoot the living hell out of all of them. And you damn well better look like you love the gun doing the killing while you're at it."

The other three men, another lawyer and two sales reps, were wise enough to keep silent. They knew their employer, a multinational gun manufacturer, was totally intolerant of so much as one negative word about guns or any aspect of their business. The three also knew that the best way to not say the wrong thing, was to say nothing.

As far as the hunting itself went though, it was already a good day for the group. The killing was way beyond their expectations. Between the five of them, they shot more than sixty of the out of season pheasants, and actually killed a large percentage of them. They weren't concerned about those that landed still alive. They were sure the coyotes would bring them to a merciful end come nightfall. And if they didn't, it was just a bunch of birds. Nothing to be overly concerned about.

When they reached the end of the field, one of the men who worked for the Track and Trail resort and lodge, who was picking up the dead birds, gave each of them a fresh, white cloth. The men took the time to carefully wipe clean their shiny new, semi-automatic, twelve gauge shotguns. Guns were, after all, the most important part of this day. And the company expected them to be treated with all due respect. The rest of the gun cleaning would be done by the lodge staff.

As soon as the guns were properly cared for, the men got into the minibus that took them to the club house. Once there, they were seated at a table large enough to seat thirty. Since they were the only hunters this day, they were the alone at the table. As they drank their cocktails and waited for their meal of pheasant, walleye fillets, and venison tenderloin, with baked potato and fried green beans, they all looked out the window to watch the river.

"I kind of expected more of a river," the leader of the five complained. "This one doesn't amount to all that much."

The waiter standing near the table, waiting to fulfill any demands the men might have, said, "It's late summer, and the rains were short this year. Normally there's more to it."

"Yeah, well, Derrick should do something about it," he said about the billionaire who had the Track And Trail resort and lodge franchise where they were. "What the hell river is it?" he asked the waiter.

"She's the St. Catherine. She's the river that supplies the water for the big refuge."

"You mean that private abortion in just south of here, that should have been put to better use years ago?"

"She is," the waiter answered, wishing he could strangle the man. He knew the river wasn't great as rivers go, but to him she was something special. He fell in love with her even before there was a refuge, when he was still a young child. He spent countless hours exploring her as he grew up, both in and out of the water. Through the years, he'd watched with sorrow the changes that had taken place. Especially after part of the refuge was sold and turned into a resort called Lands Magnificent.

Long before the waiter's memories, before the white man came, she was mostly a gentle river with few rapids. What few that existed were of short duration, and easy enough to ride, even in a small birch bark canoe.

The soil makeup of the shoreline was the same then as now, but the land was still wild. All along the river, the vegetation that grew was just the right kind to protect the fragile banks from erosion. It didn't matter if they were steep, or barely above the normal water line.

All that changed when the white man came. Along with everything else they brought with them, they brought the lust for land. They were so filled with it they took what they could wherever they could. They never thought about any problems they might create until after they completed clearing the land, right up to her banks. When they faced the disaster their rape of the St, Catherine basin created, they were all sure that the problems were the fault of nature. It seemed as if there was always some kind of natural disaster after they worked so hard to improve the land. It was as though nature had an endless supply of floods, wind, and fire. All too torment those who desperately wanted to settle in what was once a beautiful river basin.

Gradually though, after the original refuge was created and farming the marginal land proved unprofitable, and the deserted farm land was allowed to revert back to nature, the land began its recovery. Trees, shrubs, and other plant life of all kinds filled the banks of the St. Catherine, and the erosion slowed to a near stop. Even some of the former wetlands returned, and were soon filled with waterfowl.

Unfortunately, the river and its recovering basin were then discovered by hunters. It became a popular place to hunt, especially for ducks, pheasants, and geese. It didn't take long for corporations in various kinds of hospitality businesses to eye the potential of the land and river for making large profits.

Quickly, the land that was near worthless on the real estate market was selling for ever higher prices. Now, from the old farm pond that was St. Catherine's beginning, all the way downstream to the existing refuge, most of the land was owned by three corporations. Neither the condition of the river nor the surrounding environment were considered relevant to those owners. All that mattered were the animals who could be shot by hunters. And were now raised and provided by the various lodges and resorts scattered along the river.

Hunting was what drew the people and people provided the profits. Like almost everything else in America, corporate profit was what mattered most. Most of the time, it was the only thing that mattered. A private wildlife refuge downstream mattered not all. So for them, building proper sewage treatment facilities was an unneeded expense. From their point of view, the moving water that was the St Catherine would take care of the waste.

The five men now finishing up their meal and their third round of cocktails, would never in their limited thinking have considered what was happening to this environment an issue. They were simply there to hunt and kill as many things as they could with their powerful weapons. It was being done to impress a group from a different corporation. If they managed to complete the deal they were there for, it would add immensely to their company's profits. How could the water in this small, relatively unknown river possibly matter?

Before they got into negotiations about the sale of the guns, however, they were going on one more hunt. This time it was going to be deer, another animal raised only to receive a bullet from some high powered rifle. Four men from the lodge went out with them. Two were there to act mostly as servants to the men. Two local men were there acting as what the lodge called guides. What they actually did was lead the five to the place where the deer would be released as they arrived. None of the hunting that took place at this lodge was actually hunting. It was entirely a matter of shooting and killing animals raised by the lodge solely for that purpose. No one employed by the lodge, nor any of the guests, considered the treatment of the animals an issue. Animals were animals. So how could it matter that they were purposely made so confused by mistreatment, that they weren't even aware enough to run when they were released.

None of the men in the group had much training in gun handling, and were definitely not hunters in the normal sense of the word. But one of them was so excited about killing an animal as big as a deer that he was shaking. But his almost total lack of tolerance to alcohol wasn't helping any to calm his nerves. Even so, he was determined to kill one of the only three deer yearlings to be released. So he knew he had to shoot as soon as they appeared. If he waited, they might get too far away for his now blurred vision to deal with it. Even without his now impaired vision, he was a lousy shot with any gun.

The instant something moved in front of him, he raised his gun and fired. He hit his target dead center, and it dropped to the ground. There was only one problem. The target wasn't a deer. The deer hadn't even been released yet. It was the head of one of the guides. A guide who was now dead. He was an employee at the lodge. Jeffry Carro had only recently left his former job as deputy sheriff for the Clayborne County Sheriff's Department to take this job. The hours and the pay were both a lot better at the lodge.

"Oh my god," screamed their leader, "what did you do?"

Doug Welch, now on his knees vomiting, didn't answer. What he'd just done so shocked him that he dropped the assault rifle he'd been carrying onto the ground. Something that stunned the group almost as much as the shooting did. The rifle was now actually dirty.

When the people from the lodge tried to figure out what to do next, there was no discussion about calling the police. The five hunters representing a multinational corporation were quickly hustled back to the lodge. They were assisted with their packing, loaded onto a small jet and flown to the international airport south of Minneapolis. From there they were flown back to wherever they came from.

Doug Welch intermittently cried and whined about how he didn't mean to do it. When he got home, two days before his wife expected him, he had to deal with her. He her found in bed with his best friend. It proved to be too much for him. He removed one of his company's most powerful handguns from a dresser drawer, even before the couple realized he was there. He shot and killed them both. Then he turned the gun on himself.

The witnesses to the shooting at the lodge were bribed with huge sums of money to keep quiet about it. The company knew they'd only stay quiet for just so long, and that they'd all have to be dealt with sooner or later. One way or the other.

The body of Jeffry Carro was stripped completely, wrapped in an old blanket, and loaded on a single engine, propeller driven plane. Late that night the body was flown, without lights to escape detection, into Canada. There it was dumped from the plane at about a thousand feet. A slight miscalculation was made though, and rather than land in the wild country where they wanted it, the body landed in the small pasture owned by a subsistence farmer who avoided contact with other people as much as possible.

Chapter 1

The St Catherine River was low for they time of the year as she flowed peacefully through the refuge. Even so, turtles rested on rocks and logs along her banks, and frogs moved constantly in and out of the water. Ducks, geese, and other water fowl swam in ponds she provided the water for. Deer appeared there to drink before quickly disappearing back into the brush, now often high enough for them to hide in. There had been a lot of growth since the fire that burned most of the refuge a couple of years ago.

Mack and Lisa Thomas took in all the activity of the multitude of life forms that made a home in this refuge they were visiting. It was Saturday, a near perfect August morning. The temperature was in the mid seventies, and the sky was a vivid, deep blue. A perfect day to visit a wild place.

They loved it there, and were grateful they could visit when they chose to, even though it wasn't the same it once was. Only a couple of years ago, the entire refuge burned in a massive wild fire. Now it was in the recovery stage. A recovery which would take many more years. But it was a recovery that, if a person paid close attention to the way Mack and Lisa did, seemed almost miraculous.

Right after the fire, conservative politicians and various corporations claimed the fire had burned so hot that it would take a hundred years for it to recover. It should, they claimed, be sold to the highest bidder and turned into something useful. And to them, the only thing useful was something that would make some rich man richer.

It was a battle that Mack had fought for many years. A battle he, now along with Lisa, was still fighting. And now it was an even tougher battle, with nearly the entire hospitality industry demanding the the refuge be sold. There were huge sums of money to be made by providing a place for men to kill animals. The sale of guns to those men was even more profitable. Given how hard they needed to fight to save this place, where animals could live out their lives without being slaughtered way before their time, Mack and Lisa doubly appreciated a day like this.

They held hands as they walked a path that for a short time stayed close to the river. Lisa was looking up, following the antics of a pair of scarlet tanagers, when Mack made a sudden stop.

"I wonder what happened to it," he said, dropping Lisa's hand and moving next to the river.

"What is it?" Lisa asked.

"Upstream," he said, "it looks like a deer floating in the water. I'm going to try to grab it and pull it to shore. I think it'll be a good thing to know what killed it."

He was forced to wade into the river a ways, but he managed to catch a hind leg of the small deer and drag it to shore. It took no additional effort to see what killed the animal. She was littered with a half dozen bullet holes. Because they were near the north end of the refuge and the deer had been floating downstream, there was no doubt in his mind where it came from.

Poaching was an ongoing problem in the refuge. It always had been. Mack knew it would be as long as anyone, no matter their age or mental condition, was allowed to own and use guns. But this, he knew, wasn't done by poachers. This deer was from one of the hunting lodges north of the refuge.

He was further convinced of it when two more dead, young does followed closely behind the first one. Especially since they too, were riddled with bullet holes.

"It looks like," he said to Lisa, "that they're not even bothering to bury what they slaughter any more. Those lodges up north of us were already sloppy about what they allow to end up in the water. But now, dead animals?"

"Yes, and you have to be the one who found them. When it comes to the dead floating in the river, it's beginning to seem like you're cursed with the ability to find them."

"I'm starting to get that feeling too, when you add these three deer to the three women floaters I found during the floods last spring."

"Yeah. You don't just find them, you find them in bunches. But at least this time, we don't have to start hunting for murderers."

"That depends on how you define murder. And I would call what was done to all three of these deer murder."

"I won't argue with you on that. But this time we know the who, what, where, and why. With the bodies last year, we didn't. Trouble is, even though we know more, there isn't much we can do about it."

"I know, but we can watch them. Sooner or later, people stupid enough to need to kill innocent critters to find pleasure in their lives, will make mistakes. With luck, we'll catch them at it when they do."

"I sure hope so. I know the odds are against us, but I agree with you. We have to try."

"We have to do more than try, Lisa. Difficult or not, we simply have to do it."

"You're right, Mack. For the sake of this refuge, we have to do it."

That settled, they each took a hind leg of one of the deer and dragged it to Mack's truck. They repeated the process for the other two, then took the three animals to a place they could be properly disposed of.

They decided then to stop for lunch, rather than go back to the refuge. They went to a bar on the highway called the Mystic Curve Inn, found a booth, and sat down.

The young lady who waited on them knew them, so she brought a pitcher of beer and two glasses when she came to take their order, which was simple. They both ordered bacon cheeseburgers and fries.

Two men came in then, and it was obvious they'd been drinking. They stopped when one of them saw Lisa. Even though she was wearing a pair of well worn, loose fitting jeans, and an old shirt of Mack's that was too big and just hung on her, they still stared. Even with those clothes on, she couldn't hide her beauty.

Before they bothered to sit down, they approached Mack and Lisa. One of the men, the one who saw Lisa first, leaned down close to Lisa and said, "Why don't you stand up now, so me and you can have a nice dance. Be good for you to find out what it's like to dance with a real man."

"To start with, back off," she told him. "Your breath stinks. Second, I don't dance with creeps. Especially creeps like you. Third, you'd best find yourself a place to sit, or I'll probably have to sit you down myself. Getting up won't be easy if I do."

"She's right guys," Mack said then. "It'll be a much better day for you if you do. All we want is to eat our burgers in peace."

The shorter of the two men decided that it was time to prove to Lisa that he was a much better man than Mack. He grabbed his shoulder, intending to hold Mack down in the booth. It was a dumb thing to do. Mack was in much better shape than the man, and a lot stronger. He quickly left the booth, and an instant later held the man face down on the seat of the booth next to where they were sitting.

Lisa also stood up. The big man towered over her, and was about to go after Mack. "I wouldn't even think about it if I were you," she told him.

He tried to push her out of the way. With a few deft moves, she quickly had his arm bent high on his back and held it tightly, right at its breaking point.

"Let go of me bitch," he threatened, "or I'll beat the living hell out of both of you when I do get free."

"Are you really that stupid?" she asked. "Do you really believe you can do that to a couple of deputy sheriffs?"

"Deputies, my ass. You're just a couple of nobodies, and it ain't nobody what's gonna care when I do kick your ass."

"You do understand, don't you, that if you attack me when I let you go I'll be forced to defend myself. If that happens, you will get hurt, and then you will be arrested for assaulting a police officer. I will press charges, and the odds are good that you'll serve some jail time. Since you will be committing a felony, your friend here will also be charged. Do you really want to end your day in jail"

"You don't scare me, bitch. Let me go and I'll show you how much you don't scare me."

Mack decided to warn him. "You for sure do not want to try to do to her what you think you can do to her. Because if you do, you will be far more likely to end up in the hospital tonight, then jail."

The big man laughed. Lisa smiled and let him go. She stood quietly, waiting for him to make his move. He tried to grab her throat to choke her. She easily slipped out of his grasp, and slammed the palm of her right hand onto his nose. Just as she knew she would, she broke it. He staggered back from the blow, then wiped his nose with his fingers. When he saw the blood, he roared, then charged her. At the last second, she stepped out of his way. As he went by her, she clenched her hands together and slammed them with all she had onto the side of his head. He dropped to the floor.

She stood over him, using her boot to toy with his face. He was still conscious, but she was able to move his head some anyway. Then she slid it back, as if she was about to kick him.

"You had enough yet?" she asked, sliding her foot back a little more.

"I guess, for now. But this ain't over. Not in anyway is this over."

Lisa let him lay there while she put in the calls for backup. Two deputies quickly arrived in separate cars. Much to their surprise, so did Sheriff Dale Magee. The newly arrived deputies were already interviewing witnesses when he did.

"I'm surprised to see you here on a Saturday," Mack said. "Were you putting in some overtime today?"

"Yes. Trying to catch up on some dreaded paper work. So, what happened?"

"A couple of drunks looking to hassle Lisa. We were sitting in a booth, and had just ordered our bacon cheeseburgers when they wandered in. They didn't even bother to sit down before the one on the floor made his moves on her. She told him to back off, he wouldn't, she gave him fair warning, and the rest is history. And yes, we will be filing charges against them. Everything we can possibly charge them with. Including assaulting police officers."

"If you go that far, Mack, we'll have to keep them overnight. Maybe all weekend."

"Exactly. Let the assholes sit in their cell and stew over what they were trying to do when they walked in here. We are more than a little bit tired of men who think they have the right to do anything to any woman they choose to do it with. So, inconvenient for us or not, they are going to get all that the law will allow me to give them."

"Are you sure the people here will back up your claims?"

"I don't see why not. Most of the people here know us, and also know the type of men who tried the usual hassle on Lisa. When I explain to them that if they're willing to tell the truth, it'll be highly unlikely that they'll ever have to testify in court, they'll back us up."

Mack was right. Each and every person inside the bar told the same story, and the two tough guys were locked up. In separate cells. When their ID was checked out, they learned that the men were part of the management team of the Track And Trail resort and lodge.

After so many years fighting corporations and the many evils they were willing to commit in the name of higher profits, Mack wasn't at all surprised that the men who started the trouble in the bar were part of the management of a mid-size corporation. But it did make him even more determined to do everything he possibly could to put the men in prison, no matter how long or short their time inside was.

Chapter 2

None of them remembered exactly when it started, but it was now a normal thing for Mack and the rest of his family to gather for breakfast at the home of Mack's father Ben. It was an easy thing for all of them, since all of their homes were located close by, on their four hundred acre farm/ranch, not far from the refuge.

It wasn't unusual for one or more members of the family to miss the breakfast, but this morning they all were there. Also there was a woman who was a close friend of all of them. She was treated as if she were part of the family, even though she wasn't. That treatment was carried to the point that they'd bought her a manufactured home, which was setup on the five acres they gave her. Her name was Sue Sartor.

Ben's wife, Theresa had just set a plate of three eggs, two sausages, three slices of bacon, with a side of toast, in front of Mack, when his uncle Roy asked him, "How'd your visit to the refuge go yesterday. Is the recovery from the fire still progressing the way it should?"

"I wish I could say yes. But it's not happening the same as a year ago. There's a lot of pollution in the river, coming from those hunting resorts. We quit our visit early, because we ended up pulling the carcasses of three young does out of the river."

"How did they get there? Someone poaching again?"

"No, they came from one of the killing resorts."

"Are you sure about that?"

Lisa answered him. "There's no doubt about it at all. Given where we pulled them out of the water. If they would have been shot there, we would have found them way downstream. They were full of bullet holes too. Way more than what it would take to kill them."

"So they were shot, just for the fun of shooting them?"

"They were," Mack said. "All of the so-called hunting going on at those places is just killing. The animals aren't given even the slightest chance to escape the guns. The way they're raised, they don't even know enough to be afraid of people."

"All too often," Lisa said, "we don't either."

"Well," Wanda, Roy's wife said, "at least around here, because of all the work you guys and the sheriff's department are doing, women are being more careful."

"Maybe so," Mack said, "but too many men haven't learned anything about the right way to treat women. Yesterday, after we took care of the deer, we stopped at the Mystic Curve for a burger. Two guys came in right after we ordered. They right away decided that Lisa was fair game. We told them to back off, but as usual they were mighty, macho men and didn't listen. The biggest and worst of the two was especially obnoxious. I didn't hold Lisa back when she arrested him."

His last comment made all of them laugh. Lisa's abilities were well known, not only among her family, but also within all of local law enforcement. Since she decided she wanted to become a sheriff's deputy, she'd intensively studied self defense, along with all sorts of ways to take the offensive when it was required. She was also in excellent physical condition, so she was able to use all that she'd learned.

When the laughter died, Mack added, "It turned out, those two clowns are part of the management of the killing lodge called Track and Trail."

"Did you arrest them then?"

"We went one better. We threw the book at them. If I have my way, they'll spend some time in prison."

"That's a bit harsh, isn't it?"

"No, Roy, it isn't. After all that Lisa's been through in her life, she shouldn't have to be subjected to their kind of treatment, only because she's beautiful. It's a matter of enough is enough."

"I understand. I don't ever let anyone for any reason hand Wanda any shit either."

Sue, who'd been quiet so far, spoke up. "You don't let anyone mess with any of us, Roy. Not ever. If anyone ever pushed one of us too far, you'd probably break their neck."

Roy chuckled at her comments. He knew she was right, just as he knew Mack was right. Especially since the men were part of the management of Track and Trail, the killing resort he considered to be the worst of them. It was in his opinion, at best, a total abomination.

"You're right, Sue," he agreed. "I don't have any more patience for that kind of crap than Mack does."

"That's right, Roy," Ben commented. "There's other things we all agree on too. Animals should always be treated properly. The environment should be protected, instead of screwing it up the way they're trying to do in Arizona, *again*."

"What are they doing in Arizona now? Given how bad the environment's been screwed up there already, you'd think they'd finally want to undo some of the harm. Not add to it."

"It seems their Republican governor thinks too much land has been given over to things like national parks. He wants the one by Tucson, Saguaro National Park, to be sold to a private corporation that owns those resorts called Track and Trail. They think it'll be a perfect hunting place for men who want to do their play hunt in rougher country."

"And of course, none of those people involved are thinking of the environment at all. Not that it would do any good if they did. I think all of those Republican politicians studied science with Donald Trump."

"I agree," Ben said. "Which means they never studied science at all, and couldn't understand it if they did. When it comes to science, or about anything that matters, the Republicans come across as the single most stupid species on the planet."

"They go beyond stupid," Sue said. "They consistently perform more like they're insane, rather than just stupid. And as far as Donald Trump is concerned, no one has ever been able to come up with a score low enough on the IQ chart to match his. Along with the fact that he's totally evil, he is the perfect leader for those too stupid to wipe without work direction."

Her last comment brought on another round of laughter, which was followed with more serious discussion. In the end, they all agreed that the hunting resorts were almost as much danger to the existing refuge as Lands Magnificent was to the original refuge. Land's Magnificent was the corporation that managed to buy half of the original wildlife refuge and turn it into a huge resort.

Chapter 3

It was early Sunday morning, and the first rays of the sun were just peeking over the horizon. Mack and Lisa were finishing up with their horses. All that was left was tying down the saddle bags filled with the snacks they were going to eat on their planned, full day's ride.

"Are you ready?" Mack asked when they finished.

"As much as I'll ever be," she said. "I just hope that both these horses are. Even though we've been riding a fair amount lately, I'm still not sure they're in good enough shape for this long a ride."

"I think they are. We won't be pushing them at all hard, but if they do show any signs of fatigue, we can always shorten up the ride."

"I know, but I hope that today, for a change, we'll be able to finish what we've planned."

"Me too. So let's get out of here before someone comes along to change things."

Their plan for the ride was to take an old trail that ran along the St Catherine river. It traveled north, on the far side of the river from the killing lodges and resorts. Since the trail was seldom used any longer, they hoped to have a quiet, slow ride, first for the pleasure of it, and second, to check out the condition of the river.

They knew that the pollution caused by all the resorts, and the hunters who stayed at them, was now serious enough to start harming the wildlife refuge. Fish, in lakes and ponds deep enough to hold them, were already dying off in small numbers. It was obvious that it wouldn't take much pollution for the numbers to rise. So they would be looking for places where it originated, and when they found them, making note of the perpetrators. Gathering evidence against them, Mack and Lisa knew, was the only way they'd be able to force the killing places to clean up their act.

They weren't into their ride very far before their first stop. They were barely out of the refuge and near the first lodge, Track And Trail, when they saw their evidence of it. This lodge had just finished cleaning the building that housed their ducks in the winter. It was their version of spring cleaning, even though it was now well into summer.

The waste material was piled high on the river banks, so close that it was inevitable that the bulk of it would eventually wash into the river. The pen for the deer they were raising was also a source of pollution. The fence around it extended into the river, allowing the deer to drink the river water. That alone might not have been so bad, but the pen was very much overcrowded and sloped toward the river, making it a serious contributor to the pollution.

They took a multitude of pictures with their digital cameras, including closeups provided by their telephoto lenses. They even managed to get pictures and video of some of the buildings and polluting sites together, so they had further proof of who the guilty party was.

The next killing lodge was also large, and so was the pollution problem. They were dealing with the animals and their waste very much the same way as Track And Trail, so the major difference between them was the volume of waste. This resort didn't produce quite as much.

While Mack and Lisa were recording their polluting mess, an employee of the place noticed them. He watched for a while, then disappeared.

"That might be trouble," Mack said when he was gone. "So we'd better keep our eyes open."

"I agree," Lisa answered, "but there really isn't much any of them can do to us. This trail is on public land."

"Trouble is, I doubt they have any respect for that fact. So I think something else we should do is keep a blank memory card in the cameras when we aren't using them. That way, no matter what happens, we'll still have the evidence."

The ride was peaceful for the next couple of hours. The trail followed the turns and bends of the river, while it avoided hills and muddy low ground. It was an easy, altogether pleasant ride. A great place for two somewhat tired deputy sheriff's to spend a few relaxing hours.

It also was a stretch of river with low banks, so it offered easy access to all manner of wildlife that often stopped there to drink. Of the various animals they saw, the ones they found the most delightful on this ride were a pair of otters. They were playing what appeared to be a game of tag, and were in and out of the river constantly.

Lisa saw them first. When she pointed them out to Mack, they stopped, dismounted, and watched the game for a while. They held hands as they did, and enjoyed their closeness and the comfort it gave them every bit as much as the play of the animals.

Unfortunately, their serenity didn't last long. Within a short time, three men carrying high powered rifles met them on the trail. They stopped on the trail, eyeing Lisa up and down. They were there to find out what Mack and Lisa were doing, but all of them had broad grins spread across their faces. It was obvious what they were thinking. It didn't matter what their original reason for being their was. They were outside and away from anything to stop them from doing whatever it was they chose to do. From their point of view, there was little to nothing Mack could do about it, even if he did try to put up a fight. And Lisa, well, a pretty little thing like her, all she could do is let it happen and enjoy what three big, strong men were going to give her.

"Well now," the biggest of the three men said, "we've been looking for you two. It seems as though you been doing some serious snooping. Our bosses don't like it much, when people like you two do that. So we're here to find out what you're up to. But first," he gave Lisa a big, leering smile, "I think we'll have some fun with you. And there ain't gonna be a damn thing your cowboy friend here can do about it."

Lisa smiled back, but it didn't hide the hatred for them she had in her eyes. "I wouldn't count on that if I were you."

"I don't need to." He started moving toward her.

What they didn't realize, because they weren't looking and didn't expect it, was the fact that Mack and Lisa were armed. Sure what was on the minds of the three men concerning Lisa, along with knowing they were already looking for trouble, he quickly drew his gun and pointed it at the men.

"Drop the guns," he told them.

"What the hell," one of the men said, "you got no reason to try to tell us that. You got no right to either."

To prove his point, he started to lift his high powered rifle to his shoulder. Lisa fired, and the bullet whizzed inches from his left ear. She did it before he had lifted the gun high enough to use it. He didn't lift it any higher.

"All of you," Mack said, pointing his gun at the other two men, "drop your rifles now." They only hesitated for a moment before dropping their guns. "Now, you can leave your weapons where they are and turn around and walk away from us, or you can argue and spend the night in jail."

"You don't have the right to keep the guns. They cost us plenty, and we ain't done nothin' to give you reason to keep 'em."

"But you have. You've threaten both of us with violence, and you said you intended to rape my wife. So for now, I will hang on to your weapons. You can pick them up at the Clayborne County Sheriff's Office tomorrow. All you will need to to to get them back is identify them and yourselves. And there will be some forms for you to fill out so we have a complete file on all of you. That will be for future reference if we ever need it."

"What the hell do you mean, if we ever need it? Who the hell are you anyway?"

"We are deputy sheriffs. Now get the hell out of here. You can pick up your guns tomorrow."

"I seriously doubt that you are a deputy sheriff, but if you are, I'll have your job when we pick up the guns tomorrow."

Mack laughed at him. "You can try, but don't get your hopes up." Having his job threatened by men who considered themselves powerful was nothing new to Mack. It had happened so many times that it was now a meaningless threat.

He and Lisa watched the three empty handed men walk away until they were out of site. They tied the rifles behind Mack's saddle, mounted the horses, and turned them toward home. They knew that if they rode any farther that there was a good chance of someone waiting for them, hoping to get even. They'd also already ridden far enough so that the day would be close to used up by the time they got home anyway.

Chapter 4

Mack and Lisa started their day earlier than usual. They wanted to eat a normal breakfast with the family, but also wanted to be sure they were in the office when the three men arrived to pick up their rifles. For Mack, the start of the day was unusual in another way. He rarely started his day in the office, even though every other deputy was required to start their day there. It was a special deal he had with the sheriff. He got it because when he started, he worked for half pay. He still did, but now it all went to his favorite environmental organization. Mack was rich, and didn't need to draw a salary. For him, money didn't have anything to do with being a deputy sheriff.

That meant Sheriff Dale Magee was surprised to see him when he walked in. "What's going on that brings you in here this morning, Mack?" he asked.

Mack explained to him what happened the previous day. "And it turns out," Mack finished, "all three of them are employees of Track And Trail Resort And Lodge."

"That's the biggest of those places along the St Catherine River, isn't it?"

"It is, and from what we saw on our ride yesterday, it's likely it's the worst polluter of the bunch. They're all bad, but those guys are something else."

"It's kind of weird that you should happen to have a run-in with men from that place again. Friday we got a missing persons report about one of their employees. I normally wouldn't haven't given it any more than my normal attention, since he lives in a different county from ours. But he was a deputy here for a while. He quit about a year ago. You remember Jeffry Carro, don't you?" He looked at both Lisa and Mack when he asked the question.

"I sure do," Lisa answered. "He made a pass at me the one and only day we rode together. I wasn't overly fond of him."

"I remember him too," Mack said. "He was an okay deputy, but I thought his attitude could have been better."

"Well, when the three men from that place get here to pick up their guns, I'm going to talk to them about him. See if they know anything about what happened to him."

"You might get something out of them, Dale. But they didn't strike me as the kind of men who would be likely to cooperate with us, no matter what the problem is."

Dale decided to try talking to the men anyway. But even before he could ask a question when they got there, a fourth man who came in with them demanded, "I want the badges of those two deputies, and I want them now."

Dale, who's face was now filled with disgust, shook his head. "You can want anything you please. That doesn't mean you'll get it. So back the hell off. Along with the forms you're going to have to fill out to get your guns back, I've got some questions I'd like answered."

"Well that's too damn bad. I'm a lawyer and I'm representing these three men. Your deputies were way out of line yesterday. They had no right to do what they did. And for that, I expect you to get rid of them."

"It's not going to happen, so again, back off. You keep this up, and you won't be getting their guns back. Not without a court battle, and even then, it's extremely doubtful you'll get them. Our team of lawyers are anything but fond of people like you."

"You don't scare me. I can only imagine the kind of lawyers your department can afford. It isn't likely they'll know about too much."

"You think so. I'll have to let the folks at their law firm know that some of their lawyers are no good." He told them the name of the law firm. The man doing the bitching stepped back, taking a deep breath as he did.

He quickly recovered, but backed off of his demands when he spoke again. "So what is it you want to know?"

"I want to know whatever you can tell me about one of your employees. He's been reported missing. His name is Jeffry Carro."

All four of the men were surprised by the question. None of them ever paid enough attention to their employees who did the real work at their killing place, so none of them knew that Jeffry had been a Clayborne County Sheriff's deputy. So they never expected anyone in this office to take an interest in him.

They all knew how he died and what was done with his body though, and all of them were concerned about law enforcement anywhere learning the truth of what happened. Then the lawyer did his best to cover up any knowledge of Jeffry's disappearance when he answered Dale.

"We all knew Jeffry," he said. "He was a good man. One we all liked. We were definitely disappointed when he didn't show up for work one day. We never got a call or anything from him. He just never showed up. One of our guys went to his house to check on him, but no one was home."

"Why didn't you report him missing then?"

"It never occurred to us to do that. People quit jobs the way he did all the time. That doesn't mean they're missing. Is there a reason you're so interested in someone who doesn't live in your county, and no longer works for you?"

"There sure is. Before he went to work for you guys, he was a deputy of mine. He was well liked here, so we'll all be taking an interest in where he is and what happened to him."

"I wish we could help, but none of us know anything more than what I've told you."

Nothing more was said about Jeffry while the men were at the office, doing what they needed to do to get their guns back. With that task completed, they left the office secure in the knowledge that Jeffry's body was dumped up in the wilds of Canada.

They had no idea that the body wasn't in the wilds, but was actually in the middle of a pasture that was seldom visited by humans.

They also left behind three suspicious people in Dale's office. Mack was the first to comment. "They are all liars," he said as soon as they were out the door. "Especially the lawyer. I don't have any idea about how much they know about Jeffry's disappearance, but they definitely know something."

"I totally agree," Lisa said, "but I think they know more than just something. I think they know a fair amount about what happened to Jeffry when he disappeared."

"All I know for sure," Dale added, "is that there was something they weren't telling us."

"The thing I noticed most," Mack said, "was how cooperative they were after you asked about Jeffry. They're the kind of men who normally have to be pushed a lot before the back off from their belligerent nature."

"Yeah," Lisa said, "and they even eased up on their staring at me. Instead of the nasty look in their eyes. it turned into more of a worried one."

"I can't argue that," Dale agreed, "but there's not much we can do about it right now. So you guys might as well get out and about, keeping the citizens of Clayborne County safe and secure."

So they did. Lisa drove through town to start her day. Mack immediately headed to the outer parts of the county. The places with more of the wild things than people.

Chapter 5

Along with the many ways Theresa Thomas shared the work of raising a multitude of vegetables with her husband Ben, she also raised close to five hundred chickens. She marketed them as needed at the local farmer's market, and gave a lot of them away to the people she worked with at the local community garden she managed.

The garden was located right in the heart of Kingsburg, so the land it was on was valuable. That meant that a lot of business people hated to see it there, when money could be made with other uses for the land. Those same people hated her for running it, and even more, hated Mack for buying the land that was once a middle school and a football field. Turning it into a community garden was for them a travesty. The good it did for the city and the people in it meant nothing when compared to the money that could have been made by some of them from some other business.

There had even been the occasional death threats made. No one worried too much about the one's made to Mack. He was an armed deputy sheriff, skilled at his job and every bit as skilled with the gun he carried, so he was very capable of defending himself.

Theresa, on the other hand, wasn't any where as able to defend herself. Even though she'd been occasionally getting the threats for many years, for a mistake she made, currently the threats were coming ever more frequent.

The earlier threats came from her being involved with some teenage boys. When it happened, she was suffering from severe depression and other mental issues after her husband committed suicide. All those issues disappeared after lengthy treatment, then meeting and marrying Ben.

From her point of view, her life couldn't be any better than it was now, and she was thankful for it. Ben was more than a good husband. He was a kind and generous man. Of all the things he shared with her, the most important was his family.

That family hadn't just accepted her. They had made her welcome and to feel as much a part of them as any of them were. At first it seemed strange that they were so open and kind. The family she grew up in were a conservative, tightly religious bunch. But none of them ever followed those things that Jesus taught the way this family did. And with no exceptions, they were unbelievers in religion. They agreed with the teachings of Jesus, but not in the son of god stuff. And now, after listening to many conversations they had on the subject, she was now agreeing with their opinions. That new way of thinking now felt like a ton of weight had been lifted from her head, and she was now finally free. It gave her a sense of satisfaction in what she did, and a way of seeing things she had always before considered impossible.

Her positive outlook on almost everything in her life, however, meant she failed to be as careful about what and how she did things. So this night, after an unusually long day at the community garden, she failed to notice the car following her home. It wasn't until she turned into the driveway of the farm/ranch where she lived, that she noticed the car at all.

Even then, she might not have, had it not been what it was. It was rare, if ever, that a black limousine with windows tinted too dark to see through drove past. Especially one that immediately increased its speed as it went around her as she turned into the driveway.

The car only stayed in her active memory for a few minutes before she filed it in the place in her brain where those things trivial were stored. That's where the memory of the car stayed until the following morning. For her, it was a pleasant evening spent with Ben. A light supper, a little conversation about the day they'd had, and then early to bed.

She got up early in the morning too. She wanted to be sure that she could get to the garden right after breakfast, do what needed doing, and be back in time for the noon meal. Ben had a lot of picking to do in his own fields and she wanted to be there to help. Like every other member of the Thomas family, she hated waste, and she knew that if those vegetables growing so prolifically in those fields weren't picked, they could easily be wasted.

Her efforts proved fruitful, and she managed everything just the way she had hoped too. She was just getting ready to leave the garden for home when the limousine from the night before pulled into the small parking lot and stopped behind her car, blocking her way out. She noticed it, but it still didn't concern her much. Her thoughts were now focused on the work facing her when she got home, and the fact that Ben would be very glad to see her when she got there. She was sure that whoever was in the limo, would be perfectly willing to move it for her.

She didn't even see the man get out of the limousine. She was about to walk to the driver's side of the limo to ask him to move when he suddenly appeared in front of her. Startled, she gasped and snapped her head back.

"Excuse me," she said, her tone of voice now anything but friendly, "but I need you to move out of my way."

He waved the gun he was holding under her nose. It was a small caliber revolver. "Don't you remember me?" he asked. "You damn well ought to remember me after what you did to me, you goddamned whore."

When he called her that, she looked closer at him. It took a while before she recognized him. Her memories of him were less than pleasant. He was the only one she tried unsuccessfully to reject when he wanted things from her she wouldn't give him. He was one of the boys she had been involved with years ago. Like all of them, he was a more than willing participant, so she didn't understand why he was so angry. She wasn't able to stop him when she said no, but she never did anything about what he did. Evidently the look on her face was confusion, so he explained why he was there.

"You ruined my life, bitch," he whined, "when you forced me to do those horrible sinful acts with you. I lost my soul doing them, and now I'm not able to do them with women. Thoughts of you are the only thing that can stimulate me enough to be a man. I hate you for that." He started to cry. "Now you work in this garden from hell, with all these people who have lost their souls to the greed of making a garden where there should have been a church. My father's church."

He paused, then pushed her hard. She fell backwards, and on her way down, he shot her in the head. He stopped crying then, and smiled at the small red hole in the side of her forehead. She was dead, he was sure. He turned, walked to the limousine, and got in. He backed out slowly, but accelerated rapidly when he drove back onto the street.

He left town on a county road that took him to a seldom used, narrow township road. It wasn't much more than two tracks in the sand that seemed to disappear as it moved over a small hill.

His own pickup was parked there, and that's where he left the limousine, parked next to the dead body of the original limo driver. He had planned the day, and so far everything had worked out exactly as he had hoped. His pickup was packed and ready to go, so that's what he did. He left, heading directly to the four lane to begin his journey south.

He never cared much for Minnesota, so now that he'd accomplished his mission, he was extremely glad to be heading back where he was sure he belonged. Tucson, Arizona.

Never mind the heat there. Lots of people complained about that. But as far as he was concerned, it was nothing compared to the cold Minnesota was filled with seven months of the year.

No, the weather there wouldn't bother him at all. In fact, nothing would bother him now. At least now, it wouldn't if his father would finally gave him credit for doing something right. After all, by killing Theresa he'd actually accomplished two important things.

Most important, he'd rid the world of the woman who brought such a horrible sin to so many innocent young men like himself. And he'd gotten some revenge for his father's loss of the place he desperately had wanted to build his church.

Never mind that as a teenager he'd almost gone to jail for messing around with a seven year old girl. It also was irrelevant that his father could never have raised enough money to buy the land and build a church. What really was and what he and his father wanted them to be didn't have to relate to each other. Much like the religion they constantly preached. This was the America of Donald Trump, and now for so many, any kind of insanity, especially where religion was concerned, was considered normal.

And given that both he and his father were ridged evangelicals, insanity actually was normal. So he was pleased with himself now. He had performed God's will to near perfection, and rid the world of a heathen, liberal woman. A woman, from his and his father's point of view, who had absolutely no worth what so ever at all.

As far as the limo driver was concerned, what was done to her couldn't be helped. She was collateral damage, and as everyone knew, when serious activity was happening, collateral damage was permissible. And the fact that she was a woman doing what he considered a man's job, meant that her elimination was simply part of a righteous cause. And because she was invading the world of men, where she didn't belong, she also had to be among the worst of the worst. A liberal.

That, however, wasn't the way Mack or Dale or anyone in the sheriff's department looked at any of it. From the second the 911 call came in about Theresa, Dale and his department became involved in the shooting. Because it went down in Kingsburg, the city police had the lead in the investigation. But because the shooting victim was who she was, the sheriff's department was welcomed to work with the city on the case.

When Mack learned about it, he rushed home to tell Ben. He was patrolling the county within a couple of miles from home, so it only took minutes to get there.

He didn't fool around when he did, and drove right out into the field to get him. "What the hell are you doing, Mack?" he asked when Mack stopped next to him. Driving out into one of Ben's vegetable fields in a pickup truck was not something Ben would normally tolerate.

"Best get in, Dad. It's Theresa."

Ben jumped into the truck without another thought about the vegetables, and they were on their way to the hospital before he even got the door closed.

"What the hell happened?"

"She's been shot."

"Where? Why?"

"It happened as she was leaving the garden. She was shot in the head. We don't know why. We don't know how bad."

"You mean, she's probably dead."

"We just don't know, Dad. All we can do now is hope."

"Most of the time you know, Mack, a bullet in the head doesn't leave much hope. I lose her and I'll lose a lot more than just hope."

Mack knew the truth to what Ben said, so he didn't answer him. Instead, he concentrated on his driving. Something that made sense, since they were going well over a hundred miles an hour on a narrow county road with lights flashing and the siren wailing.

At the hospital, Mack dropped Ben at the main entrance, parked his pickup, and rushed inside. He found Ben talking to a doctor just outside an operating room.

"How is she?" Mack immediately asked.

"She's alive," the doctor answered. "She should be okay. It appears that the bullet went in at an angle, that didn't penetrate the skull. It did, however, travel a ways under her skin, against her skull, so she's going to be real damn sore when she wakes up. They're taking out the bullet and cleaning up the wound now. They need to be sure they get it perfectly clean, so it's going to take some time."

"When can I see her?" Ben asked.

"Not until the surgeon working on her is done, and the nurses assisting complete their work.," the doctor answered. "Even then, you'll have to wait until she's awake and we're sure she's recovering properly. You might as well take a seat in the waiting room. I'll let you know when you can see her."

Dale was already in the waiting room, and Roy and Wanda joined them minutes later. Lisa was writing a traffic ticket in a far corner of the county when the call came through, so she arrived several minutes later. Sue Sartor was picking tomatoes in a field a fair distance from where Ben had been working, and her cell phone was off when the call came through, so she was the last of the family to arrive.

When she arrived, Wanda sat next to Ben, and without saying a word, she took his hand and held it. He turned to her, and the look in his eyes was all the thank you she needed. Ben was the kind of man who could deal with almost anything, but this, what happened to Theresa, was almost too much even for him to deal with.

They were all quiet for a while. There had been too many times that they all gathered in this same waiting room, hoping that whoever it was this time, would survive the operation to remove the bullet or bullets from their bodies.

It was Lisa who finally broke the silence. "Do we have any idea who did this?" she asked.

Everyone lifted their head in response, but it was Dale who answered her. "All we know, Lisa, is that he was driving a limo, probably rented somewhere down in the cities. That's being checked out now. Someone who was in the garden got a partial plate number. The shooter wasn't wearing a uniform though, so we don't think he was the one who should have been driving. What happened to the regular driver remains to be seen."

"I imagine then, that the airport, bus and train stations are being watched."

"Yes, Lisa, all the standard procedures are being followed."

"I know. I'm sorry, Dale. It's just seems so totally wrong, that someone, anyone, would want to shoot her. If it was me or you or Mack, it might make some kind of sense. Us being cops and all. Not Theresa. She is so kind, so decent. She would never intentionally hurt anyone. So why the hell would someone shoot her. It makes no sense."

"This kind of thing never does. Never will. I just hope we can catch the monster who did this. Theresa means a lot to me too. She is, after all, my wife's aunt. Kathy loves her as much as anyone. Except Ben maybe. Not to mention how fond of her I am."

Mack spoke up then. "This is one we have to catch. Theresa means too much to every damn one of us."

"You know," Ben said, "it is important to catch the man who did this. But it's even more important that she recovers. So let's hope for that first."

They all understood all too well what he meant and how he felt, so it again became a quiet group of people filled with hope. It was a long two hour's wait then, before the doctor joined them.

"Good news," he said, a slight smile on his face. "She's out of surgery and near as we can tell at this stage, she'd going to be fine. The bullet caused some damage to her skull, but thankfully didn't penetrate it at all. But she's going to have a headache for a while that the pain killers won't be able to do much more than ease some."

"Can we see her now?" Ben asked.

"Just you for now, Ben. And when you do see her, go easy with her. Especially with the questions. She's in enough confusion already, without you adding to it."

"Okay," Ben agreed. "I'll go easy."

"I know that there are no choices about this," Mack said. "Theresa comes first. But the longer we go before we know who did the shooting, the harder it is going to be to catch him."

"We all know that, Mack," Dale said. "But it's best to wait anyway."

"It might take longer this way, Mack," Lisa said. "And it might be more complicated. But we damn well will catch the son of a bitch. No matter how long we have to wait for Theresa."

The problem then was, the wait for Theresa was longer than expected. Ben didn't get a chance to ask her any questions during his first visit with her. Her doctor chased him out of the room she was in before they had any real chance to talk.

It was evening before they let him see her again. She was still a bit groggy when he went into the room, but gave him a weak smile anyway. It wasn't until after the how are you and I love you, along with all the things people say to each other, that Ben asked about the shooter.

Theresa turned pale at the question, turned her head away, and said, "Please don't ask me that, Ben," she pleaded. "I don't ever want to talk about it. I just want to forget it."

She was filled with guilt now, blaming herself for what happened. She was sure that he did it because of what she allowed to happen all those years ago. What she couldn't have known or understood is the fact that he did it to please his father, God, and maybe even Donald Trump. After all, he was the new messiah for him, his father, and so many other millions of very sick people.

Ben didn't want to press her at all, but there was no way he could understand why she didn't want to tell him who it was that shot her. "I'm sorry, Theresa," he told her, "but I don't understand. We need to know who did this to you. He tried to kill you. When he finds out you're still alive, he might come back to try again. So you know that he has to be stopped."

"I just can't talk about it, Ben. I don't ever want that part of my life back again. Can't we just forget this happened and get on with our lives?"

Ben took her hand and gently held it. He did his best to soften his tone when he spoke to her again. "I can only guess what part of your life you're referring to. No matter what it is, if it was just up to me and you, I might let it drop. I understand how painful the past can sometimes be. But I can't do that for you now. You have to know, there's no way anyone else in our family is going to let go of this. They won't quit until one way or the other, the man who did this to you is in jail or dead."

"I just can't tell you, Ben. I feel terrible about it, but I can't talk about it. I was wrong, doing what I did. Please, let me forget it. Talking to you about it is too painful."

"Well, if you won't talk to me, who will you talk to? You're going to have to talk to someone before this is over. I love you and I'll be here for you no matter what this is about."

Theresa turned her head away. Her eyes were filled with tears. "I'm afraid, Ben. If I have to talk about this, I'm afraid that all of you will hate me. Only Mack. He'll be disappointed, but he won't hate me. I'm sorry, Ben. I just can't do this. If you want me to leave now, I don't blame you. I'll go."

Ben didn't answer her. He couldn't. So he sat with her until she slept again, and then went out to the waiting room. It was late, so everyone other than Mack, was gone.

"Did she tell you anything?" Mack asked Ben as soon as he saw him.

"She won't. She says that if she talks about it, everyone will hate her."

"Did she give you any hint as to why we would hate her?"

"No, but she did say that you wouldn't hate her. She thought you'd be disappointed, but that you wouldn't hate her."

That comment made Mack feel that there was something he needed to remember. It took him a while for his memory to open up to his early experience with Theresa. When he did, he thought he knew what her problem was.

"I need to talk to her, Dad. Alone. I'm pretty sure I know why she doesn't want to talk."

"I'm pretty sure I know what the shooting relates to," Ben said, "but I still want to know the answer for sure. You know I'll stick by her no matter what. Are you going to fill me in on the problem if you get some answers?"

"It'll be up to her to how much I tell you. If she asks me not to talk about it if she tells me, I'll give her my promise. I won't lie to her anymore than I would to you."

"Is there a reason you won't tell me now, before you make the promise?"

"Yes, there definitely is."

"And that reason is, Mack?"

"The deep respect I have for your wife. I don't want to upset you, but I won't hurt her, even for you. She's just too special."

Ben looked into his son's eyes. He knew then that it would be wrong to argue with him. So they waited until they felt she'd slept long enough. Without waiting to get permission from the doctor, Mack went into her room this time.

He gently touched her shoulder to wake her. Her eyes slowly opened, and when she saw him she sighed heavily. "I suppose you're here to get me to talk, Mack. I'm sorry, but like I told your Dad, I can't talk about it. It's all my fault anyway."

"The hell it is. You've never done anything to deserve this. I'm pretty sure I know what this is about, so you don't have to explain anything to me. What you do have to do is give me his name if you know it. I promise you, I won't talk about this or tell anyone what's behind what happened. If possible, it'll never get talked about, but I can't guaranty that. As far as what happened way back when, you didn't really do anything particularly bad then. You're way past being to blame for any of it now. They were teenage boys. About as innocent in their behavior as Trump is in his. Which is to say, they definitely were not.'"

"My god, Mack, if only everyone was as kind and understanding as you are, life would be so much easier. But I'd still rather not talk about any of it. And them being what teenage boys are, doesn't make me any less guilty."

"The thing is, Theresa, you might as well tell me. Because even if you don't, I will find out who did it. There weren't that many of those boys. And if I have to learn who did it that way, I'll be asking a lot of people a lot of questions. That will make it much more likely for everyone to learn what it's about than if you just tell me."

"But why do you have to? Why can't you just let it go. I don't need revenge."

"This isn't about revenge. It's about the law and doing what's right. It was right back then when you weren't arrested, in spite of what some people wanted. And now, it's right that we catch the man who shot you, before he hurts anyone else. Even if you look less than perfect in the process. Besides, you are now part of a family who loves you one hundred percent, and will continue to do so no matter what."

"If I do, you'll try to keep from telling anyone what started this, what made him shoot me?"

"I will. But what made him shoot you isn't what you think. He did what he did because he's just another nutcase with a gun. A nutcase who shouldn't have been allowed to have a gun." Mack stopped his comments there. He could have talked for a long time about guns and the people who shouldn't have them, but knew he had to focus on the problem with Theresa while he had her attention.

"Okay, Mack. I'll tell you. Since I first met you, you've been nothing but kind to me. You've trusted me when it appeared to everyone else that you shouldn't. So now I'm going to trust you. His name is Todd Baker. I don't think he lives in Minnesota any longer. He was abused as a child. His father frequently whipped him for committing one sin or the other. His family was extremely ridged evangelical. He was the only one of those boys who tried to force most of what happened. It was my fault for allowing anything to happen, but he was different from the rest. No matter what he was involved in, in school, he always seem a little bit off."

"Thank you, Theresa, for telling me. You've saved me a lot of time and effort. It was the right thing to do."

"You have to know, Mack. I wouldn't have told anyone else. Not even your dad. But you've given me your trust sometimes, when even I'm not sure you should have. For that, I owe you. I'll always owe you."

"The only thing you owe me," Mack said, smiling now, "is to be good to my dad. And speaking of him, I'm going to get out of here and send him in. I know he's more than a little anxious to get back in here."

"I have a name," he told Ben as soon as he saw him. "And she wants to see you, so you'd best get in there."

"Are you going to tell me what and how, or not. I couldn't get a damn thing out of her."

"The what is that she really loves you and the how is just that sometimes things just work out the way that they do. But right now, I've got to run. I've got a real bad person to find and arrest."

"But, Mack, I'd like…"

"Maybe sometime, when it's all over, I'll tell you. But then, don't hold your breath."

Ben just shook his head as he watched his son walk away. He wanted to know more, a lot more. But like his wife, there was no one he trusted more than Mack. Because of that, he could leave it in his hands, without knowing for sure, the what and why. At least for now.

Chapter 6

Mack knew when he left the hospital that the quickest way to put together preliminary data on Todd Baker was to sit down at a computer, and using the resources available on the internet, do a search on him. But while his was at the adequate level on the computer, he had someone to go to who's skill went beyond even being a usual techie. She was one of those people that could accomplish things that would be impossible for the average computer user, even if they had a hundred years to learn the techniques.

If Mack was any deputy other than himself or Lisa, he would have been forced to ask one of the deputies in the department who was proficient enough to do the search. Since he had his own specialist, he went home to get the job done.

When he pulled into the driveway, instead of going home, he turned onto the one leading to Sue Sartor's house. She opened the door for him on the first knock.

"Mack," she said, looking somewhat surprised, "what brings you here?"

"I've got a name. I need you to do a search on him."

"I hope you've got more than a name. No matter who it is, there could be a lot of people out there with the same name. But before you do that, call your wife and tell her that you are here. Neither one of us needs to have anyone wondering even in the slightest amount, why you are here."

"But, Sue, you know our family isn't that way."

"Yes, I most certainly do. But I want to keep them just like they are. Call Lisa."

He did, and she laughed when he explained why. "I knew you were there, Mack," she said, "and figured it was something like this. You and Sue can do your search on that guy now. I'll see you when you're done."

Mack turned to Sue when he finished with Lisa. "She laughed when I told her I was here. She already knew, and wasn't concerned."

"I didn't really think she would be. I just like keeping things on the up and up. I love working with you. With all three of you Thomas men actually. But I have to tell you, Mack, sometimes I like it too much. So it's best for me that your wives know what we're doing when we're alone together, no matter what we're working on."

Mack took a momentary mental step back as he realized what Sue just told him. Her words were a big surprise. She had always hidden her feelings toward him, Roy, and Ben so well that he'd never suspected anything like that from her. She gave him a moment to absorb it, then further explained why she did it.

"I wasn't ever going to say anything about my feelings to you or Ben, even if Roy does know about them. But I did it, because it's getting ever more difficult to hide them. Wanda knows, and I'm sure that Lisa suspects, so I think it's time it's brought out into the open. That way, there'll be far less chance of any of us acting on those feelings. Also, as much as I love it here and love being part of this family, if this situation ever starts to upset Lisa, Wanda, or Theresa, I will leave. I don't ever want to, but I owe too much to all of you to stay under those circumstances."

Mack shook his head. "I don't know what else to say, other than I'm flattered. As for you ever leaving here, as far as I'm concerned the only reason would be if you got married. Then it would be only if your new husband insisted."

"I'm glad you feel that way, Mack. I only ask now, that you and Lisa talk about it, and that she's still okay with me being around."

"Okay, I can do that."

"Good, now tell me what you can about the man you want me to research."

Mack told her everything he knew about him. She quickly followed it with checking everything she could find out about him, from the time he was born at the Kingsburg hospital, all the way through his buying a house in Tucson.

Actually, his father bought the house for him. It was more than he could ever have afforded on his income as a busboy at the local strip joint. The house was on the east side of Tucson. It was located on Broadway, a relatively busy road with a lot of retail businesses that catered to the middle class.

Only two years before his evangelical preacher father bought him the house, he would have been able to purchase it himself. But with the rapidly growing real estate bubble, prices were now completely out of site.

The one thing they hoped to find, which there was no evidence of, were some kind of travel arrangements. No tickets on the bus or airlines from either the Tucson or Phoenix's bus stations or airports. They also couldn't find any fuel charges on any of his credit cards. So they couldn't find any proof that he'd been in Minnesota. That meant they'd have little to no chance of convincing Tucson authorities to arrest him.

It was a big disappointment, but an even bigger disappointment was the fact that Sue dug up his connection to Theresa. Now Mack was faced with explaining to Theresa why Sue now knew about the part of her past she would have preferred to keep private.

He knew that Sue wasn't about to lay any judgments on Theresa. She would never even bring up the fact that she knew. But sooner or later Theresa would learn that she knew. Mack knew that it would be less upsetting for her to find it out now than it would be later.

It was late by the time he left Sue's. His head was aching and his brain was in a turmoil when he did. His first concern was Theresa. He knew it was going to be difficult explaining to her how he'd already let her down, so he was dreading that chore.

Second to that was the question about how to handle the situation with Todd Baker. The last thing he could do was to do nothing. The man had to be brought to justice. The question was how. It would involve traveling to Tucson, he was fairly sure. What to do when he got there was something else. Something he would have to start figuring out in the morning.

The last of the many things jumping around in his brain were Sue's comments about the way she felt about him, Roy, and Ben. There was no way he would want her to ever leave her home. She was too much a part of the family now. Yet, at the same time, he was a bit worried about the possible conflict if anything ever happened between her and any of them. He was carrying a big frown when he got home.

"And what is wrong with you, Mack?" Lisa asked as soon as she saw him.

"I'm not sure you want to know."

"Oh, come on now, it can't be that bad." She followed the comment with a hug and a kiss.

It was enough to convince him to answer her. When he finished his long explanation, she told him, "In the first place, we all already know about Theresa's past. We have all along and none of has ever judged her for it. I think you need to explain that to her. If you do, I think she'll get over her current fears.

"As far as Todd Baker is concerned, you and I are going to drive to Tucson, figure out a what it'll take to arrest him, and bring him back here for a trial.

"And Sue is no problem. Us Thomas wives have known for a long time how she feels about you guys. Given that we are lucky enough to be married into this family, none of us can really blame her. She also is highly unlikely to ever do anything out of line. Add to that, the fact that all of you guys are straight arrows, I think the best thing we can do is forget about it. It's something we all can live with."

Lisa fed him supper then. It came right out of the refrigerator, into the microwave, and on to the table where he sat and ate it. It actually wasn't bad, he decided, given it was originally cooked to be eaten about three hours earlier. Mack wasn't about to complain about eating a warmed over supper. Getting home as late as he did, he didn't feel like he had any right to. Not after she'd put in the effort to make the meal even though she too, worked all day.

While he ate, then rinsed his dishes and put them in the dishwasher, she showered and went to bed. He followed her there after his shower, and was surprised to find her awake.

"I think," she said, "what I want now is something Sue can never have."

And then he was thankful for such a good end to such a bad day.

Chapter 7

Larry Jameson was a bit of a recluse. It wasn't so much that he hated people as it was that he just didn't have any time for them. Most of them, in his opinion, had so much more than they needed or could even possibly use, yet what they did most of the time was bitch and complain about what a hard life they lived.

He also considered that most of what they did was a waste of time. He thought people who spent hours every day, sitting in their over sized cars to go to do a job they hated, were at least partially crazy. For him, the thought of living in a city was something he never wanted to dwell on. It would be a life that was simply too horrible to live in. Too much like that of a caged animal. For him, life required that he always be free. Something that required that he aways live alone. He knew that even if he did someday find someone to love, they wouldn't be able to share life as he intended to live it.

His life was basically self sufficient. Simple, and because he loved his way of life, it was for him easy. He had a large garden, a fruit orchard, and he kept a few animals for milk and eggs. He hated killing animals, so he stopped eating meat of any kind when he was still a young man, barely out of high school.

Most of his animals were kept close to home, but he let his three milk goats use his small pasture during the warm months, which didn't last that long in this part of Canada. His chickens made use of the pasture too, as did his aged horse. An animal he only used once a year to plow his garden. The fences around the pasture were old, but solid. He only took the time to walk around them to check them once or twice a month.

He normally didn't pay much attention to any of the pasture, other than the boundaries and the fences located there. The horse kept the grass short enough to be comfortable to walk on, yet long enough to remain healthy and green. This morning though, he couldn't help but notice a spot in the middle of the pasture where the grass was taller than the rest. Even some of the goats favorite plants were taller than they usually were allowed to grow.

It was obvious that the goats and the horse were staying away from the spot, but most of the chickens were hanging out there, doing those things that chickens do.

At first Larry ignored the spot, but as much as he tried to continue to do so, his curiosity got the best of him. He walked over to see if there was something special going on there. There was, and he nearly lost his breakfast when he he saw what it was.

Laying there was the remains of a naked man, no longer quite complete. The chickens, along with other wild creatures, were obviously feeding off him. What stood out the most though, was the massive damage to his skull. A large chunk of it was missing. It was a wound that was very unlikely to have been made by any kind of animal.

Larry didn't have a phone, cell or otherwise, so he was forced to drive the fifteen miles to the nearest town. It was not something he wanted to do. He and the local police did not like each other at all. It was seven years since the dislike started, but the cops still carried their grudge toward him as strong as ever.

It only took one incident to cause the problem. Larry was relaxing with a beer in the local tavern after a day of shopping for his winter supplies. A guy sitting in a booth next to a very pretty, but very young lady, suddenly went berserk and pulled her out of the booth. He hit her in the face with his fist, knocking her down. When she didn't get up right away, he kicked her.

That was enough for Larry. He went over and told the kicking man to stop. The guy responded by taking a swing at Larry. He landed a glancing blow, but that was the last thing he did. Larry's fighting skills, learned while serving his country, far surpassed those of the kicker.

He could have taken the man down with a single punch, but he was angry now. When he finished with him, his face looked similar to corned beef hash. The problems Larry ran into then were two. The woman the kicker was going after was his new wife, and he was a cop.

If there hadn't been so many witnesses willing to testify on his behalf, Larry would definitely have gone to jail. For this particular police department, getting away with beating one's wife was far more important than anyone's rights.

And now Larry had to face them, knowing that nothing about the department had changed. When he went inside the police station, the cop at the desk there shook his head in disbelief.

"I don't know what you're doing here," he told Larry, "but if you're smart you'll turn around and take it somewhere else."

"I would if I could. Trouble is, I can't do that. I'm here to report a dead body I found. I thought you might want to know about a dead body."

"If you're the one who made it dead, I sure would."

"Sorry, no, it wasn't me."

"So, where the hell is this dead body?"

"In the middle of my pasture. I found it a couple of hours ago. It's been there a while."

"In your pasture. That tells me it's likely you who put it there."

"I'll tell you what. Before we go on with this bullshit of yours any further, start acting like a cop instead of the first class asshole that you are. If I was responsible for a body in my pasture, why the hell would I be here now? All I would have to do is bury it and you would never in a million years know about it. So now, what I want you to do is get the person in charge of this place, so I can tell him about it. I damn sure don't plan to waste any more time discussing it with a person who has your level of intelligence."

Strangely enough, the cop left his desk and did exactly that. The man he brought back said, "so what's this about a dead body in your pasture?"

"That's what it's about. There's a dead body in my pasture."

"So, how long's it been there?"

Larry answered all the man's questions. "You mean to tell me then," the man said, "that today was the first time you've been out in that pasture in near a month."

"That's exactly what I'm telling you. Other than checking fences, I don't have any reason to go out there."

"Okay. I think your story is pretty far fetched, but I'll come and check on your body. Give me directions on how to get there."

When the cop arrived at Larry's, he brought someone else along. He was a doctor, and the local coroner. Contrary to the local police department, he had a decent education and was very good at his job.

After a preliminary examination of the body, he told the cop, "I have no doubts that this is a homicide. And from the looks of it, this isn't where it was committed. It all actually looks strange to me. I'm going to get a forensics team here to check this out."

Larry knew then that he'd done the right thing by reporting the body, instead of just burying it as he was initially tempted to do.

The forensic team, when it came the next morning, spent several hours at the sight. It was late in the day when the body was finally removed. As everyone was getting ready to leave, Larry asked about what they'd learned.

"We don't know anything with an absolute certainty. It's possible that we never will. What we are fairly sure of though, is that the man you found was shot in the head. Probably with a high powered rifle. There's no way to be certain how he got in your pasture either, but If I was to guess, given the condition of the body, that it was from the air."

"Is there anyway you can tell me once you know?"

"Normally, we wouldn't do that, but given that you did the right thing by reporting it, and the fact that this is a strange one, I'll do my best to inform you."

"Thanks. I'd really appreciate it."

Larry was surprised then, when the cop shook his hand and said, "From now on, if any of my officers give you a hard time, let me know. It took guts for you to come in and report this. I admire you for that." The cop was grinning when he walked away. Not only did he appreciate what Larry did, he was happy about it. It gave his department something way beyond the normal day to day to do.

It also gave a lot of people in law enforcement, both in Canada and the United States, a little extra work to do. And as it so often happened, a lot of the fell on the shoulders of Sheriff Dale Magee, Detective Paul Danielson, and Mack and Lisa Thomas. Even so, it wasn't any of them who actually solved the mystery.

Chapter 8

After they gathered all the necessary information on Todd Baker, Dale convinced a judge to file all the papers needed to arrest and extradite him from Arizona. Then he contacted the Tucson police to let them know Mack and Lisa were going to be picking him up. They decided to drive, to have some relaxing time, but also to avoid the problems with carrying weapons through airports and on planes. They also felt like there would be somewhat less hassle to transport Baker than it was by air.

When Mack and Lisa finished planning their trip to Tucson, Arizona, they loaded Mack's pickup with everything they thought they'd need. They were ready to leave the following morning.

During all the years he followed rodeo, it was Mack's habit to start any trip, no matter how short or long, in the early morning hours. This trip though, Lisa suggested that they eat breakfast with the family before they left.

"There's no reason to be in such a rush," she told him. "Dale told us we could take whatever time we needed, and we do have plenty of legitimate vacation time built up. So it only makes sense to eat breakfast with them. You know as well as I do, that we won't get a breakfast that good again until we get back home."

"I know," Mack agreed. "And you're right. We aren't in that big a hurry. So it doesn't matter how I used to do it, this time we'll travel however you want to."

As things normally went, Roy was the first one to say anything when they got to Ben's to eat. "You guys are ready to go then," he said.

"Are you looking forward to the long drive and hot weather when you get there?"

"I would be," Lisa told him, "if we were going there for a vacation, instead of a hunting trip. Given what we'll be doing when we get there, I don't expect this trip is going to be very fun filled."

"Lisa said it about right," Mack agreed. "As far as the drive down goes, it should be interesting. Traveling always is, if you pay attention. As far as the weather goes, it doesn't matter how hot it gets, it won't match the misery of a typical Minnesota winter. The trip, I think, will be a mixed bag. No matter what we're facing, we'll get some good out of it."

Theresa, home from the hospital now, spoke up then. "No matter what," she said, "I don't want either one of you doing anything dangerous. I know you're making the trip to get the guy who shot me, mostly so he can never do it again, but you're too important to get hurt because of it."

Mack had told her that everyone in the family had known about her past already, and was pleased at how well she was dealing with it.

"We'll be careful," Lisa answered, smiling. "Getting shot or otherwise hurt, isn't something either one of us enjoys." That reminded everyone that getting shot was something both Mack and Lisa were familiar with.

Talking about the fact that Mack and Lisa's trip could prove to be dangerous cast a worried shadow over their conversation, but they managed to change the subject for the rest of the meal.

That didn't change anyone's concern though. When they finished eating everyone left the table when Mack and Lisa did, and walked them out to the pickup for a final goodbye. Lisa especially appreciated it, yet at the same time felt a tinge of regret that she wasn't doing the same thing with her family. But her reasons for not doing it were simple. To save them the worry. All she told them was that they were only going to Tucson for a much needed chance to relax.

After all the goodbyes were said, and Mack and Lisa were finally on their way, she took one last look at everyone as they drove away. They all had smiles on their faces. But everyone of them had eyes filled with concern. Too much happened to both of them in the past, for anyone waving goodbye to believe where they were going was safe place to be. Lisa sighed heavily when she turned her head away.

"I know," Mack told her, "it's hard to leave them behind when they're all so worried about us. But given what that nutcase did to Theresa, it is important that we make this trip."

"It is that. And it damn sure isn't something we could ever let slide. Not given who we are and where all of us fit in the community where we live. But that won't change the fact that I will worry just as much about how they are doing as they will about us."

Mack couldn't help smiling at her words. "Of course you will. That's who you are. And that's the way our whole family is. Both sides. Your's and mine."

They grew quiet then, and by the time they past Minneapolis and the southern suburbs, Lisa was asleep. The scenery in southern Minnesota was nice enough, but the constant hum of the tires and the sameness of the freeway, was hypnotizing. Even the rolling hills in Minnesota and Northern Iowa weren't enough to hold their interest.

Mack stopped at nearly every rest stop before his first stop for gas outside of Des Moines. Lisa took over the driving then, and after that they changed off about every two hundred miles. The worst part of the drive was going through Kansas City, where they managed to arrive during rush hour. Lisa happened to be driving, and she hated every minute of it.

She lived her entire life in Clayborne County, and had little experience with traffic like Kansas City produced during its rush hour. So it was a white knuckle ride for both her and Mack. He drove from there all the way through the Kansas turnpike.

From the turnpike they picked up highway 54, which was much more to Lisa's liking, given it was a two lane with reasonable traffic. A short time later they stopped for the night. They stayed in a decent motel with a fast food hamburger joint next door and a service station not too far away. they gassed up before checking into the motel, then got takeout hamburgers and fries for supper. That meant they were ready to go as soon as they woke up in the morning, which they did very early.

When they reached the town of Tucumcari, highway 54 followed I40 for several miles. As soon as they entered it. Lisa was more than happy that Mack was driving. Even in those early hours of the day, the freeway was almost bumper to bumper, and made up of trucks. It wasn't that long a drive, but even with all his driving experience, Mack was more than happy to leave that stretch of freeway.

They continued to follow highway 54 to Alamogordo where they picked up highway 70. It took them to Los Cruces, which was a city. Lisa was driving again, and not at all happy about it. They were forced to detour for some construction, and got lost because of some bad signs.

They found their way to I10 anyway, but Lisa pulled over shortly before she entered it. "I need to stop driving for a while," she told Mack. "I know I haven't driven my share this time, but I think you'll do a much better job of it right now."

"That's fine, Lisa," he said. "All that construction was a bitch to get through. I'll take the rest of the way if you want."

"No, just let me relax for a while."

The traffic on I10 proved to be only moderately heavy all the way to Tucson. They made their last rest stop at the rest stop in Texas Canyon and marveled at the rock formations there. They didn't need to fill up until they reached Tucson. Mack was still driving when they did.

They left I10 while they were still on the east side of Tucson, because that was where Todd Baker, the man who shot Theresa, lived. It was late by then, so they decided to find a motel for the night, and start their investigation in the morning.

Because they were in Tucson, they ate supper in a Mexican restaurant, and had an excellent meal. Mack especially enjoyed the fact the there were so many extra side dishes to go along with his fajitas that his order filled two large plates.

Mack showered first when they got to the motel, and was relaxed on the bed, wearing only a pair of shorts when Lisa came out of the shower. She had a towel wrapped around her and was wiping her hair dry with a second towel.

Mack took one look at her and said, "Wow. When you look like that, Lisa, you make me feel like the luckiest man on earth."

She smiled, took a couple of more wipes on her hair. and dropped both towels she was using on the floor. "I'm glad," she said, and crawled on the bed next to him. Before they slept, she once again proved how lucky he actually was.

It was early morning before he stopped holding her. When he did, she gave him proof again. Then they slept until the hour was decent enough to pay their visit to the local police.

They were hoping that the police had already arrested Baker, but they hadn't as yet even made any attempt to.

The officer at the desk in the police station explained why. "Like too many police departments, we're somewhat understaffed, so we only provide that service to the most serious cases. Usually just murder. So you are on your own as far as picking him up goes."

"You have no objection then, to us picking him up and transporting him back to Minnesota."

"None. And you shouldn't have any problem with him either," he told Mack. He eyed Lisa up and down. "Considering the great help you've got with you."

Mack shook his head and glared at the cop. "It never ceases to amaze me, the amount of ignorance some cops have. She is the best damn partner any cop could have."

"Oh, I don't doubt that, but how good is she if the shooting starts."

Mack knew any further discussion with the cop was futile, so he took Lisa's arm and led her out of the station before she killed the man. "I'm sorry," he said, "but I think we'd best just find our guy and get him back home. It just ain't worth it, to get into any fights with these cops."

"I know, Mack. But damn, I sure would like to get in a ring with that jerk. Even if I couldn't beat him, I could still teach him a thing or two."

"I have no doubt about that at all."

From the police station, they drove directly to Todd Baker's home. Mack sent Lisa around to the back door of the house, then knocked on the front door. After several tries, he was fairly sure the man wasn't home. He thought about breaking the door down, but decided it would be best not to. At least, not on the first try. So instead, they went door to door and questioned several of his neighbors about him.

Mack was aware of the fact that some of them might warn Todd that someone was looking for him. But he figured that whatever information they might learn about him, would make it worth it to take the chance. The problem there, was the fact they didn't learn anything new.

To fill the time they would have to wait before they tried to find Baker again, Mack took Lisa to Sabino Canyon. It was a popular tourist attraction, but was also used heavily by the locals.

The canyon itself was surrounded on both sides by high cliffs, and was filled with a large variety if dessert plants. They took the tram ride to the end of the canyon, and they found the ride to be extremely scenic. Then they walked back down.

In Minnesota it would have been an easy walk. In Tucson, because of the heat, it proved to be a fairly long walk. If they'd have known they were being watched closely every step of the way, it would have seemed a lot longer.

Todd Baker knew who they were as soon as they got out of Mack's truck when they stopped at his house earlier. He stayed out of sight when Mack knocked on his door, then followed them when they left. He even managed to ride the tram to the end of the canyon without them seeing him.

Normally, either Mack or Lisa would have noticed him fairly quickly. But because they were now beginning to relax and feeling close to a vacation mood, they weren't being near as vigilant as they should have been.

They tried twice more to find Baker at home, but had no luck. By then, they were beginning to feel the frustrations that went along with trying to find someone in a city they knew so little about.

They ate Mexican again that night and retired early. For a lot of people, their evening could have been boring. For Mack and Lisa, their long evening stuck in a motel room proved to be quite the opposite. They were relaxed now, more than they'd been for a long time.

Chapter 9

Todd Baker went directly to his father's new church when Mack and Lisa went to their motel. As he always was, he was impressed with the size of the new church, located in a strip maul. It was in an old supermarket. The building's size was nothing compared to most of the newer superstores, but was fairly large for its time.

Todd was also happily surprised at how well his father was doing with his preaching. It was very different than what it was when he was growing up and the evangelicals weren't near so popular. Now though, the nonsense they preached went along perfectly with with the Trump worship and his nonstop hate speech. Not to mention the lies and constant nonsense coming from the entire Republican party.

The best thing of all though, as far as Todd was concerned, was the fact that his father was making a lot of money. That meant he could afford to support Todd. That left Todd, who hated work of any kind, free to pursue his passions. Passions that included murder, attempted murder, and raping women, no matter what their age.

The problem now though, was Mack and Lisa Thomas. He didn't actually know Mack at all, but he knew Lisa. They were in the same class in high school, and although they never knew each other socially, he knew a lot about her anyway. Especially the fact that she, along with Mack, was a deputy sheriff.

Now they were here in Tucson looking for him. He had no doubt that they were there because he shot the bitch Theresa. The woman who wouldn't let him do to her whatever he wanted to do to her. It might have been a long time ago, but he still hated her for rejecting him and his nasty, mean advances. As far as he was concerned, she was a whore and should have done what he wanted, no matter what it was.

So now he needed to figure out how to deal with them. He hoped his father would have some answers. When he explained the situation to him as they talked in the church's rather plush office, his father, Joseph Bakker, had a quick solution.

"It's simple," he said. "I'll give you enough cash to see a friend of mine. He deals in guns of all kinds. Buy yourself a high powered rifle with a scope and kill them."

"But where can I do that?"

"Your problem, not mine. Now get out of here. I have some church business to attend to."

Joseph gave his son a few thousand dollars and walked him to the door of the office. As Todd walked out of it, a young girl of about fifteen walked in with an older woman. The girl looked nervous. The woman looked pleased. She knew she'd be paid well for this one.

Todd was disappointed by what he saw. He would have liked to stay and assist his father with the urgent church business. With either the girl or the woman. He wasn't fussy.

Instead, he left to find the man with the guns. The sooner he completed his business he was sure, the better he would feel. And he did. Just holding the AR15 in his hands made him feel powerful. About as manly as he could ever feel.

When he drove far out into the desert to sight in the scope to ensure its deadly accuracy, he came close to a climax from just firing it. He knew then, that when the bullets landed in human flesh, especially Lisa's, he would go over the edge without even touching himself. So it was with a great deal of excitement that he thought about the how and where he would shoot Mack and Lisa Thomas.

Chapter 10

Dale was surprised to see the caller ID on his phone. Why would a forensics lab in Canada be calling him. "Is this Sheriff Dale Magee," the feminine voice on the other end of the line asked him when he answered.

"It is."

She identified herself and said, "This is a courtesy call. Is Jeffry Caro a former deputy of your department?"

"He was, and he's been missing for a while. I sure hope you are calling to tell me he's been found."

"He has, but the news isn't good."

"Has he been injured? Or worse, is he dead?"

"The latter, I'm afraid."

"Can you tell me what happened to him, and where? I know it must be in Canada, since that's where you're calling from."

"It's more complicated than that. His body was found in a rural area. It was a small farmer's pasture actually. He was murdered. Shot in the head. The trouble is, that's not where he was killed. After a lengthy investigation, we have concluded the the body was dropped in the pasture from the air. We identified him from his DNA."

"And that means," Dale said, "that the murder could have taken place anywhere, including here in Minnesota."

"Yes, it could have. And to tell you the truth, that's part of the reason we're being so courteous with our notification of his death. We are hoping you can help us some in solving this crime."

"I'll do what I can. Do you have any idea what kind of gun was used to kill him?"

"There's no way we can be absolutely sure, but our best guess it was a high powered assault rifle at relatively close range. A lot of our conclusions are based on experience as much as science, but we don't think that it as a traditional murder. We think it looks more like a hunting accident that someone for some reason wanted to cover up. So the body was dumped where it was. We're also fairly sure it was dumped at night, and landed in that pasture by accident. They were probably hoping to dump it somewhere in the wilderness."

"That's as awful lot to come up with from a dead body in a pasture somewhere. But it does give me something to start with. He was working for a local hunting lodge when he went missing. That's too big a coincidence to let slide."

"I agree," she said. "Way too big." She gave Dale the name of their local police chief and his number. "It will be greatly appreciated if you will keep him informed of whatever you learn from your investigation."

"I will do that," Dale agreed. "And I appreciate you calling to inform me about Jeffry Carro. We've had an interest in what happened to him since we got the missing person's report on him."

As soon as he hung up the phone with the lady from Canada, he sent a text message to Detective Paul Danielson to come to the office at his first convenient opportunity.

When Paul got there, Dale told him about the phone call, and after a short discussion they decided to pay the management of Track and Trail a visit. As was normal for them, the first person Dale and Paul talked to when they got there was anything but friendly.

"I don't know a damn thing about Jeffry Carro," the stubby little man answered. "I've got a hell of a lot more to do than worry about lowlife employees who don't show up for work."

"Is that the way you think about all your employees?" Dale asked. "Just a bunch of lowlifes? Is that why he was killed? Because he was such a lowlife?"

"What do you mean, killed? I ain't killed nobody." He tried to snarl, but swallowed heavily. "Ain't nobody here killed nobody." He looked down at his desk, not wanting to meet Dale's eyes.

"Well," Dale answered, "I guess that's something we'll have to check into. But for now, I want to see your manager."

"He won't want to see you. He doesn't like cops. You guys do nothin' but try to take a man's guns. Guns we have every right to own. It says so in the constitution."

"Call him anyway. Tell him we want to talk to him."

The man made the call. "He said to tell you," the man said after he hung up with the manager, "that unless you got some kind of warrant you can just get the hell off this property. He has no intention of wasting his time with you."

When Dale didn't immediately answer the man, Paul did. "Tell your manager for me, for us, that he just made a huge mistake. Most of the land this *place* uses for your so-called hunting is in Clayborne County, even if this part of your butcher business isn't. That means, we will be watching you real close. You and all the people who are ignorant enough to stay here to do their so-called hunting."

"Cop or no cop, you can't be harassing our guests. You do, and we'll slap a lawsuit on you."

"Well, you can maybe try. But that whole lawsuit thing is a two way street."

"In this case it's not. You've got nothing you can sue us for."

Neither Paul nor Dale bothered to answer. Instead they both laughed. It was bitter laughter, but laughter nonetheless.

"Now that was a classic exercise in futility," Paul said. "Just a total waste of time. And as obvious as it was that he was lying, I doubt we'll ever get the truth out of him or anyone else in this organization. The only good thing about today, is the fact that they've made it obvious that we should keep an eye on them."

"I know," Dale agreed. "But no surprise. Not given the way these people make their living. I'm sure there are some places like this that are legitimate, and there's actually some real hunting available, but this isn't one of them."

"No, it damn sure isn't. But sick as this operation is, I think the people who use it for their so-called hunting are just as sick. Why the hell would anyone want to come here just to kill some innocent animal?"

"That's something that I can't even begin to answer."

"Me either. But one thing's for sure. When Mack and Lisa get back from Tucson, they'll be wanting some answers. So it'll be best for us to learn as much as we can in the meantime."

"It probably is, but it'll be a plus to have them working on this with you. It always seems as though the answerers come quicker when it's the three of you together."

"I couldn't agree more. They've become two very fine cops in less time than most of us could ever think of. And even though both of them have been to hell and back, they're still such good people."

"Yes they are. I wonder how they are doing right now?"

Chapter 11

Mack and Lisa were up and out of their motel room very early their second morning in Tucson. Before they considered eating breakfast or doing anything else, they drove to Todd Baker's house. As they did before, Lisa watched the back door while Mack knocked on the front door.

When Todd saw who it was at the door, he immediately tried to escape out the back. In his rush to get away, he forgot to check for anyone waiting for him there. As he went out the door he saw Lisa, but ignored her and the gun in her hands. After all, she was just a woman and couldn't defend herself against a big man like himself. And as for her gun, she couldn't possibly have the courage it would take to shoot him.

Lisa, however, did have the courage to shoot him. She also hated him enough to put the bullet in his head when she did it. But she also knew how much hassle and harassment she'd likely have to go through here in Tucson if she did, so she made a quick decision not to.

Instead, as he tried to race by her, she used a couple of deft moves and took him out. She was cuffing him when Mack joined her in the back. She gave Mack a small smile. "Almost seems too damned easy," she said. "I've had females who were a lot more difficult to take out than this asshole."

"I don't doubt that," Mack said. "Chickenshit's like this one rarely put up much of a fight. I doubt that this creep could last against you in a fight much longer than about five seconds."

"He couldn't, that's for sure. But let's get him to to the police station so they can process him the way they wanted to. The quicker we get him there, the quicker we can be on our way home with him."

"I agree that we should take him there right away, but don't be in quite so big a hurry to leave Tucson. There's a lot here to see, a lot I'd like to show you. So this afternoon, I think we'll take a hike up in the Rincon Mountains. They're in the east part of the Saguaro National Park. We've already got the hiking boots, and we'll stop and buy a couple of backpacks to carry water on the way there. This is one place where you don't want to go on any kind of hike without water."

"Okay, Mack, I'll try to relax and enjoy our free time here. I know you're anxious to show me around, since you've been here before. And a hike in the mountains sounds like fun."

"Yes, I have been here, more than once, when I was riding rodeo. It's been a few years, but I don't think things have changed all that much."

When they turned Todd Baker over to the Tucson authorities, they were confident that he wouldn't be any kind of trouble while he was being processed through the system. They were wrong.

When he made his one phone call, he called his father, Joseph Baker. His father then called their lawyer. The Lawyer, using cash he got from Joseph, managed to find a judge who was more than willing to grant an immediate bail hearing. Given the fact that the judge was also a member in good standing at Joseph's evangelical church, bail was immediately granted. Jeffry was again a free man.

Once he was out of custody, he had only one thought in mind. To find and kill Mack and Lisa. He started hating them just for who there were. Now, after what Lisa managed to do to him and the nanes they'd both called him when they caught him, his hatred had doubled. Finding them, he was sure, shouldn't be all that difficult. After all, they didn't realize it, but they told him where they'd be. He too had hiked parts of the Rincon Mountains, so he was sure he would find them. And when he did, he was going to delight in the surprised look he knew he'd see on their faces just before they died. And after they did, maybe another trip to Minnesota would be in order. He now hated the entire Thomas family. And none of them would suspect a thing.

That thought was one of the few things Jeffry was ever right about. No one did suspect or expect anything from him, since he was supposed to be locked up with the Tucson Police Department.

Because they felt secure in that knowledge, Mack and Lisa drove to the parking lot at the end of Speedway and started their Rincon hike with no thoughts but to enjoy it. Once they started out though, Lisa became curious about Mack's previous hikes there.

"When you hiked here before, Mack," she asked him, "did you hike alone or was someone with you?"

"What made you ask that?"

"I don't really know. The question just popped into my head. I kind of thought you'd just say that you were alone."

"Why would you assume that?"

"I guess because you've done so much all alone in your life. And you often seem to enjoy your lone hikes in the refuge."

"Does it matter to you though, Lisa, whether I hiked here alone or with someone?"

"Not really, but I'm starting to wonder now, why you seem to be defensive about it. I'm not trying to pry, Mack, so if you don't want to talk about it, we certainly don't have to. But it's not like you to not want to answer my questions. Especially questions as simple as this one."

"It's not that I have something I need to defend." Mack stopped and looked into her eyes. They were now showing a bit of concern over the conversation they were having. "I just don't want to talk about something that might bother you."

"Why? Did something bad happen here?"

"No. Definitely not bad. Not here anyway. My last hike here is one of the best memories I have of all the times I was a rodeo cowboy." He started walking again.

"What made it so special?"

"Who I was with."

With that answer, Lisa couldn't stop the slight feelings of jealousy creeping up on her. "Whoever it was, she must have been someone special."

Mack stopped walking again. He turned to Lisa, touched her under the chin to lift her head, and kissed her. "She was very special, Lisa," he said when they broke the kiss. "But she isn't anyone for you to ever be concerned about. No one and nothing will ever change the way I feel about you."

Lisa felt reassured from his words, but the feeling of her needing to know who it was that was with him, overcame the feeling that it would be best to let it go. "I'm sorry, Mack," she said, holding him tight against her, "but I will feel better if you will tell me who it was."

Mack shook his head slightly. This wasn't something he wanted to talk about with anyone. Even with all the years between then and now, all those memories, both good and bad, brought a deep sadness that he knew would never completely leave him.

Seeing those feelings deep in his eyes made Lisa realize that it would have been a lot wiser to have not asked any of the questions she'd just asked him. "I know," she told him, "that you can't forget that I asked so many questions. But you can for sure forget about answering any more of them. I'm sorry that I asked."

Mack swallowed hard, took a deep breath, and answered her. "No, Lisa, I'm sorry. I should have told you about this a long time ago. I was with my wife, Julie. It wasn't long before she was killed. I loved her very much, so losing her was something I will never get over completely. But that doesn't mean I love you any less."

"I wish there was something I could do to make it better for you."

"You don't have to. You do it everyday, just being you. But memories like that don't go away. I don't think they should either. I think we should remember better than we do, the people who pass through our lives. Sometimes, I think, we try too hard to forget. It's part of why we screwup so often."

Knowing how right he was, Lisa just took his hand and they continued up the mountain trail. She felt bad about putting Mack through what she'd just done. She knew he'd had more than his share of tragedy in his life, but she also knew that it all had made him stronger, and a kinder, gentler person. Once again, she was reminded how lucky she was to have him so much a part of her life. But the melancholy feelings they both had slowly faded as the trail grew steeper and ever more rocky. Their concentration now went primarily to the trail they were on, with little left to dwell on their conversation. Other than an occasional stop to look around at the scenic views around them, they put everything into the hike they were taking.

What they noticed most was how the saguaro cactus, so plentiful where they started, thinned out steadily as they claimed higher. Those cactus, more than any other plant life, defined the Señora Desert. Along with the saguaro cactus, they also were paying more attention to each other than to the rest of their immediate surroundings. Lisa often took Mack's hand, wanting to feel him close more than anything else.

On one of their short stops, as they look around, Lisa said, "It's almost impossible for me to believe that anyone would want to turn something as beautiful as this is, into something specialized in killing animals."

"I know," Mack said. "It used to affect me that way too. But I've been fighting those ideas too long. The one thing I've learned along the way is the fact that all too many of us care about nothing but money and power. And the only way they feel the power they want is when they harm or kill something or someone."

Because of their thoughts about that, something they otherwise should have noticed startled both of them. It took them a moment or two to realize that a collard lizard had jumped only a couple of feet in front of them. As their breathing gradually returned to normal, they couldn't help admiring the beautiful little animal standing so proud in the middle of the trail. His vivid blue color, with the black band around his neck and yellow and blue spots on his back, he managed to look like some kind of regal king.

Not wanting to chase him away, they stood quietly watching him for nearly thirty minutes before he sauntered away at his own leisurely pace. He moved another ten feet up the trail before he left it and slipped away in some brush.

The trail was taking them through a stand of mesquite when a small herd of mule deer met them. The deer were heading in the opposite direction from Mack and Lisa, and seemed to have no fear of them. They simply moved slowly along, feeding as they went. They watched in amazement as one of the deer bit off a piece of cholla cactus and stood contentedly chewing it.

For humans who hike in the desert without paying attention to where they're walking, cholla cactus can be particularly nasty. When someone gets too close to one of them, their barbed spines grab hold of clothing, boots, and all too often what seems to be their favorite, human skin. It is always a difficult, and sometimes impossible, task to get rid of them when they get attached. So it was something to see a deer chewing on one with no negative effect.

The deer were moving slow enough, so Mack and Lisa were able to enjoy their company for nearly an hour. Along the way, they were also privileged to see several species of birds, several small mammals. and all types and kinds of bugs and insects. They even met up with a male tarantula out hunting for a mate.

Near the high point of their hike, they heard the relatively loud buzz, commonly called a rattle, coming from a rattle snake. The expected to see it soon after they heard it, but they actually walked a fair distance before the saw it. It was a large snake, curled up under a mesquite. Its head was held up high, with its tongue constantly flickering in and out. On its other end, its tail was frantically warning them to keep the hell away from it. Which is exactly what they did.

They didn't walk very far beyond the snake before they started to move down. It was an easy hike there, with a wide, smooth trail. Without any conscious effort they picked up their pace along this stretch. That caused them to move up close to a large reptile sashaying down the trail ahead of them. Initially they were going to walk around it, but when they got to close, the animal had other ideas about what they could, would, or should do.

It suddenly spun around facing them, leaving no doubt that it held absolutely no fear of them. Rather, it was quite obvious that it was prepared to take on either one, or both, of them, if it decided it was necessary.

Lisa grabbed Mack's hand as she watched it. She didn't know what it was, but she had little doubt that it was a creature who was best left alone.

"It's a gila monster," Mack told her. "It won't bother us if we leave it alone, which we for sure will do. It has a poisoned bite, and if it gets hold of you, it won't let go. So be careful you don't get close to it."

"Believe me, Mack, when I tell you I won't. That thing is even scarier than the snake was."

"They can be that. It's not as dangerous as the snake, but even so, I think we'll just walk behind it for a while. Hopefully it'll leave the trail so we can get past it without any argument with it."

The fierce lizard continued to stare them down for a while before turning around and heading down the trail. It stayed there until it narrowed, then left it and disappeared among the tall grass growing there.

From there the trail they were following down became ever steeper, rougher, and rockier. Enough years had gone by since Mack hiked the trail, so he'd forgotten what a tough hike it was. It was difficult going up or down. They were in a spot where the trail was extremely narrow, with a relatively steep cliff going up on their left, and a rock strewn ravine on their right. Just as Lisa was maneuvering down a large rock, a shot rang out. the bullet hit the cliff close to them and splattered the side of Mack's face with rock fragments.

Lisa was startled enough to lose her balance. She momentarily teetered there, but lost the battle and fell into the ravine. The only thing that could be called good at that moment was that she managed to catch a branch and stop her fall before she was hurt more than some heavy bruising.

A second shot rang out and Mack was forced to dive for cover rather than seek Lisa out to be sure she was okay. She was out of the shooters sight now, and she turned in the direction of the gunshot. When Todd Baker, who mistakenly thought he'd shot Lisa, fired a third time, she knew which direction to go to find him. She started to move that way. She wished that she could check on Mack, but was sure that if she tried she'd only catch a bullet, rather than be able to help him. She knew that the best way to help him was to take the shooter out.

A fourth shot indicated to her that Mack was at least likely still alive, so she pushed through the brambles and over the rocks as she steadily moved closer to the shooter.

When she got close enough to see him, she watched him for a few moments. He was concentrating on the trail where Mack was trying desperately to stay out of his sight as much as he could. That told Lisa that she could get closer to him.

He managed to get off one more shot before she got close enough to get an accurate shot with the small pistol she now had in her hand. She aimed it at his head and asked herself whether or not she should warn him and tell him he was under arrest. But she decided that they'd already done that once, so she decided that since he was the useless life form that he was, she'd warn him her way. She also knew that a warning could put both her and Mack in more danger.

She pulled the trigger, putting a bullet into his head. He died instantly. She then called out loudly, "Drop your weapon, Todd. You are under arrest." She then fired a second time, hitting a tree trunk near where his head had been. Her bullet lodged in the tree nicely. She knew that she would be the only one to ever know which bullet she fired first. All the evidence pointed to the fact that she fired in total self-defense. That would save her the hassle of explaining why she didn't actually give him any warning.

It took a while for everything to get sorted out, but in the end the Tucson police didn't even bother to dig the bullet she shot into the tree to check it against her gun. They all agreed that she'd killed him in self-defense. It was also obvious that not one member of Tucson's investigating team that cared that Todd was dead. Especially after they heard the reason for Mack and Lisa being there.

As much as it angered Mack and Lisa, nothing was ever done to the judge who set Todd free. No one ever bothered to check the connection between him and Todd's father, Joseph.

That was what Joseph expected and wanted. He also wanted Mack and Lisa dead for what they did to his son. But during the entire investigation, he pretended to hold no animosity against them.

Mack and Lisa stayed in Tucson for a couple more days, at the request of the local authorities, but the shooting took most of the joy they might have had visiting Tucson and more of the desert.

Even so, they did spend a day at the desert museum, drove up to Mount Lemon and Summer Haven, and took one more tour of Sabino Canyon.

When they finally headed home, they took a different route, so it was freeway nearly all the way back to Minnesota. They managed to go by Denver on I25 during rush hour, and Lisa was driving. It wasn't as bad as Kansas City was, but for her it was white knuckle driving anyway.

"You know, Mack," she told him, "getting into gun battle up in some mountains might be dangerous. But I think this is worse."

He just laughed, and took over the driving at the next rest stop. They crossed Nebraska on I80, which like the stretch on I40 going to Tucson, seemed as though it was built for trucks. Not the most pleasant of drives.

They had planned to make a second stop somewhere along I80 to sleep a second night, but Mack was driving and wasn't particularly tired. So he kept on driving. Before they realized it, they were traveling around Des Moines, Iowa. From there it was a straight shot up I35 to Minneapolis.

Mack just kept on driving. It was late when they pulled into their driveway, and by then Mack was tired. They decided to leave everything in the truck and unload it in the morning. Lisa showered first when they were getting ready for bed. She was sound asleep when Mack joined her in bed after his shower.

Chapter 12

In the morning, Mack called Dale on his private cell phone to tell him that he and Lisa were back, and that they'd report in later that morning. Dale told him that they should take their time, and to call later when they were ready to come into the office.

When they dressed, it was like any work day would have been, so Lisa was in uniform. They quickly unloaded Mack's truck, then walked to Ben and Theresa's for breakfast. Like most mornings, they were the last ones to arrive.

The family was all smiles to see them. Theresa especially. She gave both of them a big hug, but Lisa got held longer than normal. Then Theresa said, "I'm so sorry that I put you in a position where you had to shoot that man."

Lisa surprise everyone with her answer. "Don't be. Contrary to what I've been told, I don't feel one damn bit bad about killing him. He was as much a low life as a human can get. He tried to kill you and then us. The world is a better place without him."

The room got real quiet for a minute or two, then Roy spoke up. "I think, Lisa," he said with a bit of a smile on his face, "that you have become a damn good judge of character."

Ben added, "I whole heartedly agree with that. If he would have stayed free there's no way any of us could be sure what he would have done next. You protected all of us when you did what you did."

Everyone was shaking their heads in agreement after that. Lisa appreciated the support she was getting, but didn't want it or their thanks to be blown out of proportion. So she gave them a simple thanks, then said, "I'll have two eggs, hash browns, two slices of toast. and whatever meat you've got in the frying pan."

That was all it took to bring them back into their normal morning conversation. It was a good thing, because by the next morning, a normal conversation at breakfast was going to prove difficult.

After they finished eating, Mack again called Dale and told him they were on their way into the office. They both drove, since they intended to go on patrol the same way they always did, which was each of them on their own, after they finished their meeting with Dale.

Because Mack and Lisa had already filed a detail report, using Lisa's computer online, covering the events in Tucson, most of their meeting was about recent activity in Kingsburg and around the county. Dale concluded the meeting by telling them about finding Jeffry Carro's body and what little they'd accomplished in their investigation about it.

"So when you two are out and about serving and protecting our county, try to keep an eye on anything and everything happening with those gun happy killing lodges. I don't expect you to solve the mystery of what happened to Jeffry Carro, but whatever you learn will be a help."

They both assured Dale they would keep their eyes open for any suspicious activity, then left the office. They were anxious to get back out and on their normal patrols, yet at the same time hopeful the rest of that day, along with the days ahead, would be relatively quiet and in general peaceful.

Their hope was lost less than an hour later. Mack's went first. Someone in a foreign made pickup moved in behind him as he started to patrol along the county road that ran along the eastern edge of the Clayborne Wildlife Refuge. It was following closer than Mack liked, so he pulled over to the shoulder to let it past him.

The problem was, the man in the passenger seat reached out his window and started to fire at Mack as it went by him. The man was a terrible shot though, and all he managed to do was make a huge mess out of the cab of Mack's truck. Mack's only injury was a cut in the face from some flying glass.

Mack didn't let the men in the truck get away. He was a superior to the driver in the truck in front of him, and he knew the road much better. It was mostly straight, so Mack was able to drive with one hand while he pulled his own gun out of its shoulder holster.

He fired a couple of shots into the rear window of the cab and the truck swerved hard to the left. It rode the left shoulder until it hit a farmer's mailbox. The mailbox had been hit intentionally before, by teenagers out joyriding, so the farmer had piled some rather large rocks around the base of its post. Hitting the rocks was enough to grab a front wheel and turn it sharply to the left. Since they were moving at just over ninety miles an hour at this point, the sudden sharp turn caused the truck to flip end from end about four times. By the time it stopped, the cab of the truck was completely crushed and the two men inside were dead.

Lisa wasn't quite as lucky as Mack. Without any kind of warning, her windshield suddenly exploded. The bullet that caused that, kept moving and lightly clipped her right arm. She managed to stay aware enough to see a foreign made pickup with two men in it race past her. It quickly made a spinning U-turn and moved up behind her.

Like Mack, she was the better driver and knew the road far better than the driver of the truck behind her. She also had a far more powerful engine in her truck, so she took full advantage of the fact. She quickly put some distance between herself and the men chasing her.

As soon as she rounded enough of a curve to put herself out of their sight, she did what they would have never expect her to do. She did her own U-turn and headed back toward the two men. She laid the gas pedal to the floor and was moving over a hundred miles an hour as she approached them. Her actions left them so stunned they had no idea what to do, so they stopped in the middle of the road.

When she got close enough to them, Lisa braked hard, and slowed enough to get a decent shot at both of them. She didn't kill them. She didn't even try. But she emptied her automatic, that she'd taken out of her holster, through her now shattered windshield and her open side window as she whizzed by them. Half of the dozen bullets from her gun hit the men somewhere.

When she called for backup, the woman who took the call said, before she did anything else, "Oh my god, not you too." After she gave the woman all the information required, she asked what she meant by her comment. "I hate to tell you this, Lisa, and maybe I shouldn't, but not five minutes ago we got the same kind of call from Mack. I'm pretty sure he's okay, but someone definitely tried to kill him.'

That left Lisa in a seriously worried state. She was tempted to call back to find out where Mack was so she could go to him, but talked herself out of it. Desperate as she was to see him, she knew the best thing she could do was stay where she was so she could assist the people who would be investigating what went down, in any way she possibly could.

She thought then, about the men she shot who were still in their truck. The most humanitarian thing she could do would be to check on the to see if she could help them. She knew she'd shot both of them, so they would be bleeding, but then remembered that they were still armed and had made one attempt on her life already.

So she decided she would try to stay safe this time and wait for backup before she risked checking on them. If that meant that they'd bleed to death, that's what it meant. She just couldn't make herself believe they were worth her dying for.

The men were still alive when a couple of other deputies checked on them, and the ambulance crews who hauled them to the hospital managed to keep them alive on the ride there. The doctors worked on them for a few hours to stabilize them, but said that they'd be a very long time recovering. Their blood loss was maximum what it could have been without killing them, so their chances of having some brain damage was high. That was something no one would know for sure until some time after they were already in prison.

Neither Lisa nor Mack had serious wounds, and both were patched up and allowed to go home. Dale told them to stay there until their pickups were patched up enough to drive. Something they didn't have to do for very long. The insurance company declared them to be totaled, and new trucks were ordered.

Dale told them that it since they were overdue for taking some time off anyway, they should stay home until their new trucks were delivered to the dealer and setup for police work.

This time neither Mack nor Lisa disagreed with Dale. They both felt as if they'd been shot at enough for a while. They were anxious to find out why the men in the pickups tried to kill them, but knew that was going to be difficult. Two of the men were dead, and the other two were no longer able to speak well enough to deliver a coherent sentence. The trucks they were driving while they made their attack were purchased, rather than rented. They were paid for with cash, so nothing connected with them provided any information on the four men. The men themselves were carrying false ID, and their fingerprints were not found in the database. So they all knew that it would be a long haul before they learned the who and what about the attempts on their lives.

They didn't like the negative result of the search for answers about the attempts. If it did have one good, all be it small, thing about it, it was that it helped convince Mack and Lisa to take the time off while they waited for their new trucks.

The first thing Mack did during his off time was check with the insurance company on the final status of their old trucks. Since they were considered totaled, the company was planning on junking them. So it was easy for Mack to buy them back at a good price. They looked like hell, but they still ran just fine. He had them taken to a body shop to be patched up enough to look more or less decent and be safe to drive. The plan was to keep them around the farm/ranch for use by anyone of them when a heavy duty, four wheel drive pickup was needed.

Filling the rest of their time off was easy. The work needing to be done dealing with their cattle was always endless, and Ben had no trouble putting them to work picking the vegetables now maturing in his fields. In between the various jobs everyone in the family found for them, they took several walks in the refuge.

It was there that they consistently found things somewhat discouraging. Even though it was for the main part still recovering nicely from the devastating fire that burned so much of it, the condition of the St. Catherine River was continuing to deteriorate.

That fact inspired them to take a day to again ride their horses up the river trail well north of the refuge. But this time they had the company of Roy and Wanda, who because of all the extra work Mack and Lisa were doing, felt free to take a day off.

All along the way, the evidence of the pollution from the hunting resort/lodges was apparent. "It's enough to really piss a person off," Roy said, "isn't it?"

"That's putting it mildly," Mack answered. "And the only reason for them doing what they're doing is to save a couple of dollars. Even if they were careful and cleaned up after themselves, their profits would still be high."

"Yeah," Lisa said, "and their polluting the river isn't even the worst thing they're doing. What they do to the animals they raise is about as cruel as it gets. Putting them out to be shot by people who don't know the first thing about guns. Then, dead or wounded but still alive, they're often thrown in a pile to rot. Either that, or dumped into the river."

"Unless it's a human. In that case they fly it up to Canada and dump it out of a plane, hoping it'll land in some wilderness where it won't be found."

"Do you really think that's what happened to your former deputy?" Roy asked.

"I didn't so much when we started this ride," Mack answered, "but the more I see of the way things are being done by these people, the more it definitely seems possible, if not likely."

They continued their ride then, taking photos of the resort's pollution as they did. This time they got somewhat farther than they did the last ride they made up the trail, before six macho men carrying military assault rifles, AR15.s to be exact, blocked the trail.

Roy was the one to speak first. "Now, I don't know what your problem is, and I don't really care. We are just peacefully out riding, and we don't need you *boys* in our way."

"You're trespassing," the evident leader of the bunch said. "So turn your asses around and ride the hell out of here."

"Number one," Roy told them, "we're riding horses, not asses. Not that any to you *boys* are bright enough to know the difference. And we sure as hell are not trespassing. This is state land. So we will damn sure keep on riding."

"The hell you will. You try to go any farther up this trail and we will stop you."

"Now how the hell will you do that? Shoot us in the back? Even if you tried, we'd kill all of you before you got more then one shot off. So go ahead and try."

"I don't think you know how fast these guns can fire."

"Sure I do, *boy*. I know what the gun can do. But I also know what you can't. So back off and go home to your mommy. I'm sure she's got a tit ready to feed you."

Roy started to move forward, but the six men didn't back off. That's when Lisa spoke up. "If you don't get the hell out of the way," she told the leader of the bunch, "I'm going to get off this horse and kick your fat ass."

As she expected, he laughed at her. The other five joined him. As soon as Lisa dismounted, so did Mack and Roy. The three of them handed their horses reins to Wanda. Lisa walked up to the leader and jabbed him in the chest with more force that he thought she could ever have.

He caught a catch in his breath and staggered back. "Well," she snarled at him. "Either turn you ass around and walk away, or I'll do it for you. And I won't be nice about it either."

As she expected him to do, he tried to push her back. She grabbed his arm and before he knew what happened, she had it jammed behind his back. "It's quit now," she said, "or I'm going to let you go, and then I intend to really hurt you."

Instead, he yelled at the five men who were with him. "Take them out, and get her the hell off me."

The five men did nothing. Mack had his automatic out of his shoulder holster and Wanda was pointing her thirty thirty lever action rifle at them. All Roy needed to do was glare at them to tell them to back off.

"I think," Mack said at this point, "It's time for all you *boys* to drop your weapons, and hike the hell out of here. You've been in our way long enough."

Lisa let go of the leader, who had already dropped his assault rifle. She stepped back, but was ready for any move he might make. He bent down to pick up his rifle. She gave him another push and picked up the gun for him. Then she turned and threw it into the river. He made a half step toward her, then thought better of it.

"You'll have to pay for that, you know," he said to her.

She laughed. "I don't think so. What I think is, you can't be threatening us the way you tried to do. This is public land, so it doesn't matter which one of those shit hole resorts you work for, you simply don't have the right to do it. You also shouldn't be threatening police officers on public land."

"She's absolutely right," Mack told them. He turned to Roy. "Now let's dispose of the rest of their trash." With that, he took the gun from one of the men and threw it in the river.

Lisa and Roy took note of what he did, and in not much more than an instant, all of the assault rifles were well out in the middle of the river, bouncing slowly along the bottom.

"Now that's going to really cost you," the leader said. "Those were expensive guns."

"It's not going to cost us a dime. Because there is no way, legal or otherwise you'll ever be able to force us to. So before you try to pull this kind of bullshit intimidating on us or anyone again, you'd best think about what it cost you this time. Now be good *boys* and move along."

They finally did. It was a dejected bunch who walked away with low hanging heads.

Lisa, Mack, Roy and Wanda continued their ride then. What they all had hoped would be a pleasant ride was now soured, both by the would be tough guys and the constant pollution problems they were finding that the resorts were causing. So they were all less than satisfied with their day when they returned home.

Chapter 13

Derrick James felt somewhat isolated from the rest of the men in the room. He was seated at the far end of the table from the man in charge of the meeting. He had the power to affect the life of every man there, one way or the other. Derrick, who owned the the Claybone County franchise for the Track And Trail Resort, had a net worth of somewhat over a billion dollars. But that wasn't even a large amount compared to what the man at the head of the table was worth.

Carson Chambers, who was both chairman of the board and CEO of Life's Protection Corporation (the largest small arms manufacturer in the world) had wealth far beyond what was publicly known, wasn't happy.

He made no pretense about being nice or friendly when he spoke directly to Derrick. "I hope you know," he growled at him, "that I have no tolerance for the kind of screwups you've been committing. The last thing I can afford is for any of my franchised hunting resorts or any of the weapons my company manufactures to get a bad name. So tell me how the hell you managed to get one of your employees shot with one of my guns?"

"I didn't do it. It was one of your gun salesmen who did it."

"It's irrelevant to me who did it. You were the one who was responsible for having things organized well enough so something like that couldn't happen."

"If your man hadn't had too much to drink, it wouldn't have happened."

"You supplied the booze."

Derrick knew then that no matter what he said, Carson Chambers would contradict him, so he didn't answer the last comment. All he wanted at this point was for the meeting to end so he could get the hell out of that room and go home.

Carson glared at him, shook his finger at him again, and said, "As bad as that screwup was, twice now, you've screwed up with outsiders who were snooping around. I sure as hell don't need anyone digging into all that pollution bullshit. Neither I nor my company can afford to deal with it the way tree hugging nature lovers want it done. Therefore, I expect you to put a stop to it. That is, if you want to continue your relationship with Life's Protection Company."

Derick decided it would be best to answer the last comment. "Of course I want to continue working with your company. Until recently, I have very gotten a lot of satisfaction out of managing Track And Trail. Of all my franchise investments, I consider it to be the most satisfactory."

"That's just fine and good, but what the hell are you going to do about the current problems?"

"To start with, we are going to follow President Trump's idea on how to solve the problem of people being where we don't want them. We are building a fence. We will not allow any trails, on either side of the river, to extend out of that horrible wildlife refuge. Further, in the future when we confront anyone who we consider is trespassing, if they give us any kind of trouble, we will shoot them. Last of all, we are going to sue that trouble maker Mack Thomas, his wife, Lisa, and the entire Clayborne County Sheriff's Department."

"Who the hell is going to pay for that damn fence you plan on building?"

"All of the owners of hunting lodges and resorts along the St. Catherine River have formed a group to finance and otherwise support whatever it is that needs to be done to deal with the trouble makers."

Carson sneered at him. "That's a start, I guess. But you'd best remember, if what you're doing does not solve the problem, then I expect you to take any solutions as many steps further as prove to be required." When Derick didn't respond instantly he added, "I certainly hope I've made myself clear. Because if I haven't, you need to know that my solutions to the problems might go well beyond simply buying you out."

Derrick seemed to shrink into himself as he listened. When he answered Carson, he was pale and his voice was weak, "Yes, I do fully understand what you expect. And I will do whatever it takes to bring this matter to a satisfactory conclusion."

"You'd, better," Carson grunted, "Now get the hell out of here. Go back to your office and try to find some solutions to all these problems."

It was an unhappy man who left that conference room. He didn't like being threatened at all. During his entire life he was the one doing threatening whenever any situation arose that someone needed threatening. His father was a millionaire when he was born, and throughout his entire childhood, he was left wanting nothing. Those occasions when he made a mistake big enough to get caught, his father always managed to somehow buy his way out of it. Even the time when he'd grown impatient with his high school sweetheart and raped her multiple times. His father paid the girl's father enough to convince him not to press charges against Derrick.

As an Adult, he'd invested well enough to build the three million his father gave him to start out, into a net worth slightly over a billion. Enough money to have things however he wanted them. Until now. This time he was the one threatened. And he knew, this time, he wasn't going to buy his way out of it. It was impossible for his fortune to stand up against the kind of money Carson Chamber's had.

That left him with only one realistic option. He planned to get together with the latest young lady in his life, who was also a bit of a computer geek. She could, he was sure, find the right man or men out there in the big, mysterious computer world to deal with Mack and Lisa Thomas. That wouldn't solve all his problems he knew, but it would be the good start he was looking for. He thought he would be able to buy off most of the rest of the Clayborne County Sheriff's Department.

When he arrived at his mistress's apartment he called his wife and explained why he wouldn't be home that night. His story for her had nothing of the truth in it, but she didn't really care. As soon as she hung up the phone, she undressed and got into the shower. She was still a very handsome woman, and she knew she'd have no trouble finding someone to spend the night with.

Carson Chambers, on the other hand, planned to spend another boring evening with his wife. They got along okay, they just didn't like each other very much.

Things changed though, when he got home. His wife was dressing up to go out, *with the girls,* she claimed. The form fitting red dress she was wearing indicated otherwise, but he didn't much care. She could go ahead and have her fun with whoever it was this time. He would happily stay home and have his.

He waited about fifteen minutes after she was gone, then left his house. He walked to his daughter's, which was on the same property, but about a hundred yards away. He had a key for the front door, which he used. He went directly to the living room, and found his daughter and her husband relaxing in front of an eighty inch, curved screen television. The movie playing was a romance. His son in law, Gerald Lucas, frowned as soon as he saw Carson. It was rare that he'd want anything other than what he usually came for. And Gerald always hated it when he came for that. It was something he knew he should stop, but the wages Carson paid him every month were too high for him to do it.

"Sorry to interrupt, Shanty," he said, "but something came up today, and I need to discuss it with you."

They all knew he was lying, but she left the couch and started to walk toward the hallway that led to the bedrooms anyway. Like her husband she wished she could bring an end to these visits. But since her farther still gave her nearly everything she ever wanted, she didn't seriously consider stopping anything.

By the time they reached the bedroom they always used, all the buttons and zippers on her clothes were open and she let them drop to the floor. She turned to face her father, unhooked the clasp on the front of her bra and let it drop. Her panties followed and she lay down on the middle of the bed and waited.

He took a little more time undressing, then climbed on the bed and did what he'd been doing to her since she was twelve. She sighed when she felt him, but wasn't as upset about it as she was sure she should be. It took her years to get used to what he was doing, but since she'd grown up, she'd learned to kind of like it. So she let herself respond to him, making him groan with satisfaction.

Respond or not though, she hoped he would be quick. Gerald always got upset if it took too long. But he didn't react the way she wanted, and it was over an hour before they returned to the living room and Carson left the house.

Gerald didn't say anything. He just waited about ten minutes. He stood up from the couch, grabbed her arm and pulled her up to a standing position. Once she was there, he hit her hard in the stomach. She doubled over. He waited a few moments for her to straighten up again. Then he repeated the fist in the stomach. He let her drop down on the couch.

"I told you," he whined at her, "it's one thing you doing it with him. We don't have no choice with that. But damn it all, you don't have to enjoy it so much."

"Next time," she said, spitting her words at him, "you come back there and watch. You'll see that I don't enjoy it so much."

He stared at her, "Well, I might just do that." He continued to stare at her, thinking what it would be like to watch her doing it with her father. The more he watched her, the more he liked the idea. It turned out to be something he wanted to do. That made him want to do her. So he did, whether she was in the mood or not.

As she realized what it was that was exciting him, she found herself getting in the mood. She gave Gerald no argument. For a few moments, they almost liked each other again.

Chapter 14

When Mack and Lisa picked up their new trucks, they were at the same time pleased and disappointed. The trucks were the same sturdy machines as the previous ones, and were equipped with the most powerful V8 Ford could install in a F250 pickup. The rear portion of the cab was close to comfortable to ride in, if the distance wasn't too far. The driver's seat was designed for maximum comfort.

The truck's had one feature not found in any normal Ford, F250 trucks. Neither Mack nor Lisa ordered it. Dale did, and he pushed the county into paying the extra cost. They were equipped with bullet proof glass all the way around. As far as Dale was concerned, they'd suffered enough flying glass.

He hated the way it seemed as though they were almost always under fire, and this was one of the few things he could do to make them safer. The only other thing to do would be to curtail their activities. That, however, would be extremely difficult, if not impossible. Neither Lisa nor Mack would ever agree to it. They were Dale's best deputies, and to not let them get out and be as involved as they constantly were, was probably as unfair to the community as it would be to them.

So they didn't make any kind of an issue about the glass, even though they found the fact that they were the only people in the sheriff's department with bullet proof glass in their windows to be unfair to everyone else. Overall though, with one exception, they were more than satisfied with the vehicles. The exception was the electronics they came with. The display on the dash had the usual radio along with the police radio, GPS, and controls that could be tied into a cell phone, making it hands free. But it also had options for many other things it could do that neither Mack nor Lisa had ever dealt with.

They gave Mack the feeling that driving his new truck would be more complicated than using a computer ever was. They lucked out though, and the dealer had a salesman who was an expert with all the new electronics, and he walked them through it. He also promised to be available to answer any questions whenever they needed questions answered.

So after half a day at the dealers learning about their new trucks, Mack and Lisa finally were able to get out and about patrolling Clayborne County. This was the work they loved, and the work that made them continue to want to be deputy sheriffs.

As they normally did, they split up, with Lisa patrolling Kingsburg itself, and Mack out in the more distant reaches of the county. It didn't take long for both of them to see some action. Lisa's call came in first. It was a domestic disturbance. Neighbors had called in and reported a violent dispute between a husband and wife. When she arrived, she found the wife laid out in the front yard, her head bleeding profusely. Her husband was standing over her, slowly delivering one kick after another to her ribs.

Lisa didn't bother to screw around with the husband. When he refused to stop the kicking after she ordered him to do it, she walked up to his six foot frame and pushed him away. He went nuts. He couldn't in any way tolerate a small, female cop pushing him. It just didn't fit into his own personal image of himself being the big strong macho man he thought he was.

He stepped in close to her, trying to hit her in the face as he did. He, of course, missed, and she landed a solid punch to the soft gut he was developing. He sucked in a couple of deep breaths to recover from the blow. As he did, he lunged at her, trying to grab her so he could hold on to her with one arm while he beat on her with his other one.

Lisa was rapidly becoming tired of his nonsense, but also felt like this might be a good time to teach him that women were not put on earth just for him to abuse. So every time he tried to grab her or hit her, she punished him. Using her feet, elbows, and the sides of her fists, she bruised and slammed his face and upper body. It wasn't until he was bleeding from his mouth, nose, ears, and both eyes that she relented and knocked him out.

The wife wasn't nearly as seriously hurt as she could have been. Before she got into the ambulance with her husband. she screamed at Lisa for picking on him.

The backup team who arrived after she called for them, interviewed several neighbors who had witnessed Lisa subdue the husband. They were all in general agreement that Lisa was justified in what she did to the man, and that she had not used any weapon when defending herself. Everyone in the sheriff's department knew that Lisa could have ended the incident quicker than what she did, but understood why she didn't. And over half of them wished they could have been the ones to deal so effectively with the husband. Lisa was back on patrol a short time later.

Mack's problem came a little later. A mother staying at the Lands Magnificent resort with her daughter called to complain that four young men had forced her daughter into their condo, and even though she was screaming, they wouldn't let her out.

They opened the door for him after he knocked and identified himself. They said they'd talk to him, but they wouldn't let him in. The mother had told him that she was underage, sixteen to be exact, and that no matter what, she didn't belong in there. So Mack told them that they'd best move out of the way. They were in enough trouble, without interfering with his investigation. Again, they refused.

He heard the girl whimpering and considered that to be enough reason to push his way in. She was stretched out on the couch in the condo's living room. A young man was on top of her, and what he was doing was obvious. She didn't seem to be doing anything to object to what was happening her, but that didn't matter to Mack. She was under age and the man she was with definitely wasn't.

"That's enough," Mack told him.

"Screw you, cowboy," the man said. "It ain't enough until I've finished what I started."

"That's right," said one of the three half dressed men standing around Mack. "And it ain't gonna be done till we say it's done."

That was enough for Mack. He grabbed the man on the couch by the hair and pulled him off it, then dropped him on the floor, using the palm of his strong right hand to do it.

One of the three standing men took a swing at Mack, which he easily ducked under. He came up quickly, his left fist landing solidly under the man's chin. He went down hard and stayed there. The two who were left tried to jump Mack. He faked a step back, ducked low, and drove his fist hard into a man's gut. As he bent over Mack locked both fists together and slammed them down on the back of his head.

The last of them started to back away, holding his hands out like he had no intention of attacking Mack. Fear was written all over his face. Mack glared at him and asked, "How old are you?"

"Nineteen," he answered, a smirk developing on his face.

"She is only sixteen." Mack said.

"So what. She's still just a whore."

That was enough. Mack hit him once, knocking him out.

"It sure as hell didn't take you two long to get involved in things that might be a problem," Dale said when they met for coffee at Katy's Kafe the next morning. "Did it?" His eyes moved from Mack to Lisa.

Lisa, definitely not in the mood to be lectured for beating up a man caught abusing his wife, said, "No, it didn't. But that's the culture we live in now. What he was doing is something I do not, nor will I ever, tolerate. So before you start on me about it, just remember that I know you're wrong for doing it."

Dale shook his head, then turned to Mack. "I expect you feel the same way, Mack," he said, "about the mess you were involved in?"

"Yes, I damn sure do. As far as I'm concerned, those four guys are lucky I let them off so easy."

"Easy, Mack. You knocked out three of them and broke the fourth one's nose. I don't think that was exactly easy."

"There were four of them gang raping a sixteen year old girl. Do you really thing I could have stopped them just by talking." Mack scowled and shook his head hard. "If you really believe that, Dale, then you've been behind a desk way too goddamned long."

"I agree with Mack," Lisa added. "You've been behind that desk far too long. The time that you get back out there a lot more than what you have been, is past due." Without consciously doing it, she glared at Dale. "At time's like this, it seems as though you've lost touch with the real world we are living in today. Mack and I know that incidents like we were involved in yesterday are getting increasingly violent. But that sure as hell isn't our choice. All we can do is the best we can with what we have. If we weren't doing that, I would have shot that son of a bitch yesterday."

"The trouble is, Lisa, it looks like our department, along with the county, are going to be sued over it."

"So, let them sue. Do yo really think there's any judge or jury who will believe I beat him up for the fun of it."

"Well, did you?"

"Definitely not. I admit I probably could have taken him out of it sooner, except he had every advantage. He was bigger, stronger, and grossly outweighed me. So I didn't take him out until I was absolutely sure I could do it safely."

"If he had so many advantages, why is he beat all to hell and you are pretty much untouched?"

"I'd guess it's probably because I'm the better fighter."

"And that's the problem. You are well trained, he isn't."

"If he wants to continue beating his wife, then he'd best get some training. Because if I catch him doing it again, he'll need it.

Dale turned to Mack. "Do you feel the same way?" he asked.

"Absolutely. There is no way you can expect us to go into situations like that and not be prepared to defend ourselves."

"Well, I hope you both realize that I don't expect that at all. The problem is, the county board is going to want to lay out some sort of punishment to appease the people and their lawyers who are suing us. I expect that they are going to order me to suspend both of you indefinitely."

"I think they will too," Mack answered. "Just keep it in mind that if you do suspend us, we will both quit. We won't miss our salaries, and we both damn sure have plenty of other things to do."

"What the hell is it you would do If you quit?"

"Work the ranch. There's always plenty to do there. We might also open a private detective agency. There's money to be made doing that.

Especially in local politics. We can hire ourselves out to any new people running for county jobs. I think Lisa and I will be good at digging up dirt on any of the men on the county board.

Dale couldn't help himself. He broke out laughing. "I'm sure you could," he said.

Mack sighed heavily. "Look, Dale, I'm sorry that things have gotten to this point. If I could stop all the violence, I damn sure would. I don't know if you remember or not, but when I first took on this job, I hated guns and violence. I'm still not a fan of either one. But I have learned, that on this job, I'm going to be forced to use both whether I want to or not.

"The world is changing," Mack continued, "and not for the better. Locally, the increase in crime and violence started as soon as they destroyed half the wildlife refuge to build their resort. It's gradually gotten worse, just like I said it would. And now with all the hunting lodges, which are actually just slaughter houses, the crime and violence is speeding up again.

"And even worse, look at national politics. We have what is far and away the worst president we've ever had. Trump is evil. He is profoundly stupid. He is dangerous. And he is leading a so-called political party that has now been reduced to a cult. A cult that not only preaches violence, they often demand it. So expecting Lisa and I to deal with all the violence we run into every day, in an always nonviolent way, is just as nuts as everything the shit for brains Republicans want."

"I don't expect you to be able to do that," Dale answered. "But I don't know what I can do to convince the county board to understand what it's all really about. You know as well as I do, they are Republicans, right down to the last man."

"I guess that all you can do is quit worrying about it. Lisa and I love being sheriff's deputies, but if it's not to be, it's not to be. Besides, it will be fun to dig up enough dirt on the county board members, to see them all replaced."

After what had turned into a rather long coffee break, Dale had a scheduled meeting with the country board. Before anyone on the board got the chance to say anything to Dale, he stood in front of them and told them the results of his meeting with Lisa and Mack. When he finished, the meeting was concluded without anyone saying anything to Dale. It was the last board meeting until their monthly budget meeting almost three weeks later.

Mack and Lisa were pleased with the results of that meeting, but their satisfaction was short lived. Only two more days went by before Lisa was sorely tested again.

Chapter 15

Lisa hoped it was just another traffic stop, but because there were four men in the car, she knew she should be careful. As soon as the car pulled over, she called in to report the stop. She then unsnapped the flap over her pistol, making it more accessibly if she needed it.

She approached the driver's side of the car cautiously, but as soon as she was close enough to the car to ask the driver for his license, all four doors opened and the four men leaped from the car.

Because she was aware ahead of time that this stop could be a problem, she was ready for them. She moved back away from them faster than they bailed out of the car. She had her gun in her hand before they could make another move on her.

"It would be best to back the hell off, guys," she told them. "Whatever your problem is today, I'm not in the mood for it."

"Well, girly, you might as well get in the mood. 'cause we mean to have at you either way."

"It's obvious that none of you know me. When I say I'm not in the mood, I mean exactly that. So if you're anxious to get shot, come and get me. Otherwise, get down on your faces."

The talker among the four men laughed. "You ain't nothin' but a girl, and where we come from, that makes you no kind of a problem to handle." He lunged at her. Before he could make a full step, she shot him in the leg. "Grab her," he yelled as he fell.

Lisa swung out with the pistol in her right hand, slamming it into the next closest man. The blow took the fight out of him. The third closest man now had a gun in his hand.

Before he could shoot, Lisa yelled, "Don't!" He continued to lift his weapon anyway. She shot him in the chest, but in a place she hoped would miss his heart.

It did, but it also didn't take him down. He dropped his arm when the bullet hit him, yet managed to hang on to this gun. He raised his arm again, taking aim at her, leaving her no choice. She shot him again, this time in the heart.

The last of the four hesitated when Lisa fired the first shot. When he realized what happened, he pretended to surrender, then tried to grab her when she moved to cuff him. He was far bigger and stronger than she was, so he was sure she wouldn't be at all difficult to teach a lesson. He would show her what a real man was. A beating was only the first step of all that he had in mind for her. He was going to have some fun with her too. Even if he was going to be forced to do it fast. Before he was done, he was sure, she would know what it was like to feel a real man in her.

She disappointed him. She twisted away from him as he reached for her. He was slightly off balance and she managed to grab his wrist and yank him further off balance. As he fell forward he moved both hands in front of him to break his fall. As his right arm stretched out his hand touched the pavement. She slammed her foot onto the wrist she had been holding. It snapped like a twig.

He screamed in pain, then turned to her. "I'm going to kill you for that, Bitch," He claimed. He tried to get up and grab her again. She shook her head no, but he continued to go after her anyway.

So she kicked him in the head, temporarily putting him out of his misery.

When the forensic team examined the incident and searched all the attackers, they found guns on all four of them. In their reports on it and how it went down they totally vindicated Lisa. They even added the fact that if she wasn't so outstanding at her job, she likely would have been seriously injured, or almost as likely, killed.

All of the men had records, and all of them had violent crimes in their records. The man she shot had been convicted of murder, but had escaped prison two years previous. All of them had lived in, and committed their crimes in Texas. All this information was turned over to the county board.

After they received it, they held a special meeting to decide what to do about what they called *Lisa's violent encounters.* Every one of the commissioners were males, and most of them had a strong dislike for Lisa. It was wrong, they felt, to have a female deputy in the sheriff's office who proved to be more competent than many of the males.

They also didn't like the fact that she absolutely could not be intimidated. It was something a couple of them learned the hard way when they tried to make a move on her.

Their special meeting lasted about twenty minutes. With a hundred percent agreement, they decided she was to be suspended for six months without pay. When she returned to the job, she was only going to be allowed to work in the office. No more patrol work. They all believed they could do that to her without losing Mack. He simply loved his job too much to quit over something they did to his wife. They were wrong.

Mack was fairly sure what it was about when he and Lisa were summoned to Dale's office the next day. "So," he said, "the idiots are going to force it this time. You're going to suspend Lisa. How long do they want to crucify her."

"Yeah," Lisa said. "How long are they going to try to punish me for being a competent woman in a job none of them could ever possibly handle?"

"Six months," Dale said, "and when you return to the job, no more work in the field. Office only."

Mack and Lisa expected the sentence the board handed out to be less than fair, but the duration and depth of this one surprised even them. Mack didn't even bother to complain or even say one word. He looked at Lisa, then nodded when their eyes met. She returned the nod.

As if their moves were synchronized, they removed their badges, pulled out their deputy IDs, and laid them on his desk in front of Dale. Mack let Lisa say it. "We are done. Please tell the commissioners for us that they can stick their jobs straight up their respective asses." Mack added. "That, and everything else we've been doing for this department. And, we will be doing background checks on each and everyone of them. Our findings will be published."

Dale just dropped his head. "I was hoping," he said, "that it wouldn't come to this. But it has." He leaned back in his chair. The look on his face was bitter disappointment. "I talked to Kathy about this last night. Like the two of you, I don't need either the salary or benefits from this job. Kathy's singing career has already provided enough to support us for years. Again, like you, I've continued to do this job because of a desire to make this county the best possible place to live. And to be totally honest, I really do love the job. Just not under these circumstances."

With that, he stood, removed his badge, gun, and ID, and laid them on the desk. "I think you know, Paul (Paul Danielson was the lead detective in the department) will be doing the same thing as soon as he learns the results of this meeting."

Lisa was shocked by Dale's moves, and knew she needed to speak up. "You don't have to do this, Dale. We know you love the job. Mack and I will feel the same way about you if you stay."

"I know," he agreed. "But I won't. And it's more than what they are trying to do to you, which is totally wrong. It's the wrong they do just because they have the power to do it. And it's getting worse. I know we can't stop it anywhere but here, where we live, but now it seems we can't even stop it here."

"You're right about that," Mack said. "As long as people vote the way they do, nothing's going to change. They voted for all those Republican commissioners, and now they can live with them. So, are you going to walk out of here with us?"

"Yes, I certainly am. But I want to say goodbye to everyone here as I do. Most of them have been with me since I became sheriff."

As they moved through the office, three of the older deputies who were eligible for retirement, decided it would be a good day to do it. All of them had overdue vacation time coming, so they decided that they would use it to fill in their two weeks notice.

Dale called Paul right away, so he joined them while they were still in the office. With his resignation, the department was now seven people short. Two more deputies in the field resigned before the day was over.

When the four of them left the office, they decided to to go out for lunch and a beer. Not wanting to have to deal with too many locals, they drove to the small town of Glentago, and ate in a cafe called the Hanging Skillet. It served what was probably the best bacon cheeseburger central Minnesota.

The only downside to the place, if you could call it that, was the fact that it was owned by a woman named Martha Fuller. She was an overall good person, except that she knew more about her customers and the goings on in the county than anyone else. Including the entire sheriff's department. So she was sure to be very inquisitive about their visit.

Mack was the only one still carrying a gun, and they all were missing their badges. It also was an odd time of the day for them to stop and eat. She took their orders before saying anything, but after she turned them over to the cook, her curiosity was eating her up.

Without asking permission, she joined them at their table. None of them could help their response to her move. It was just way too much of a Martha move. They burst out laughing. They knew what she was after and also knew that shortly after she learned what they'd done, the news of it would common knowledge out in the county.

Under other circumstances, they would not necessarily want the news to get out. But in this case, they all felt that it was only fair for the people in the county to know they no longer had a sheriff and that the rest of the department was seriously depleted. If anyone needed help, only the most serious problems would be handled. More than that, they wanted the county commissioners to know that law enforcement in the county was now in deep shit.

"Well," Martha said, "are you going to tell me what's going on or not?"

Since Dale was their leader until they all left the office, he told her. "We've quit the sheriff's department in protest against the suspension the board tried to lay on Lisa. There are several others who are leaving too."

"That's pretty harsh, ain't it. It's not that unusual for a cop to be given a suspension after they use lethal force. Especially when it might not have been necessary."

Her last comment was too much for Lisa. She glared at Martha. "When the hell was it?" Lisa asked. "That you got your head stuck so far up your ass?"

"No need to get nasty, Girl. I got that information directly from one of the commissioners."

Now she'd done it to Mack. "And you believed that lying sack of shit? You, of all people, should know better than that. You know, just as well as I do, that everyone of them is nothing more than a professional liar. Same as all Republicans."

"I'll have you know," she argued, "that I'm a Republican. Donald Trump convinced me of that from the get go. He understands what's going on in the world better than any man alive."

Mack, and the other three at the table, knew there were a million things to say to prove her wrong. But they also knew that it was a total exercise in futility to bother. She was obviously a true trumpy now, which meant she was both too ignorant and too stupid to put up with the frustration of arguing with her. She was no longer able to think or understand anything of value.

None of them wanted to talk to her any longer. Paul finally spoke up. "Given what you've become, Martha," he told her, "we'd appreciate it if you'd leave our table now, and let us eat in peace. And if we ever come back here, which is extremely doubtful, we would like for you to never sit at our table again."

His words shocked Martha, and her body snapped straight up in her chair. "You can't mean that. We are all friends. Why would you do this to me?"

"Because we choose not to associate with Nazis."

"I am not. I'm a patriotic American."

"We have no wish to argue with you. We only want to finish our meal in peace. So please leave."

She hesitated for a while, but finally left them. It was too late though. They'd already had a bad enough day before they went there to eat. Martha proved to be enough to destroy any joy they might have gotten from their meal. There was a lot of food left of their plates when they gave it up and got out of there.

There was a small crowd outside the sheriff's office when they got back there. The group gathered around the four of them when they got out of their car. Dale got a barrage of questions, all of them wanting to know what was going on.

He raised his hands to quiet them, then said, "If you want answers, you will have to contact the county board and talk to the commissioners about their wisdom in dealing with the people who make up the county sheriff's office. The four of us here have already resigned, as have several other members of the department. It is now extremely short staffed, as I assume it will be for quite some time. Keep your doors locked."

His words subdued the crowd enough to soften their voices. Several made calls on their cell phons to friends, neighbors, and family. Before the evening was over, the news of the resignations had spread throughout the county.

Chapter 16

By morning, all of the county commissioners were deluged with calls demanding to know what they did to virtually destroy the sheriff's department. When they didn't respond the way the public expected, their wives, children, and any other known friends and relatives started getting calls about the problem.

Before the end of the day, they all knew they had a problem they couldn't deal with using their usual lies and cheating. Even the most stupid of them, which was more than half their members, knew they were in real trouble if they didn't quickly find a solution.

The worst thing for them was the fact that they all knew the only good solution and they all hated it. To use it, they would have to admit that they'd been wrong. And that was something that all conservative Republicans found very close to impossible. But they soon realized that they needed to resolve the problem if they wanted to get reelected. And that was something they all desperately wanted. There was no other political job that provided as much graft.

Hating it, they finally called Dale to set up a meeting. The first thing they tried to do was tell him that he was the only one welcome in that meeting.

"Are you sure you want to insist I be the only one there?"

"Well, of course," he was told. "There is no way we can allow either Mack or Lisa Thomas there. After all, they are the cause of the problem."

Dale wasn't in the mood for their bullshit, and he said so. "No, you asshole, they are definitely not the cause of the problem. All of you ignorant bastards on the consul are."

"I think you'd best tone down the language, Dale, and show me some respect. I won't tolerate your insubordination."

Dale laughed at him. "And exactly what are you going to do about it?

Threaten me about my job? I have a hard time believing sometimes, what an ignorant bunch of total jerks you screwups are. You want a meeting with me, you will have a meeting with each and every one of us who resigned."

"We can't do that. We won't be intimidated by you."

"Then fuck off." Dale hung up on the man. He immediately called Mack to tell him about the call.

"What are your plans now?" Mack asked.'

"I don't have any. About the only thing I been seriously thinking about is your idea about a private detective agency. If we did it right, we could do a lot of good. And since none of us needs to make a lot of money, it would be an easier startup for us than most people."

"I've been thinking about that too. I think we should do it if we can't work things out with the county."

"Yeah, But I guess we should give them a chance or two."

"We should, but they aren't going to be happy with some of my demands."

"Really. What are they going to be?"

"First, Lisa is reinstated with a promotion to detective. The raise can be minimal. We don't need the money. Second, a union as soon as the people in the department vote one in. We all, and that includes you, need protection from their whims and demands and just plain stupidity. A union is the best way to do that."

"What else do you want?"

"An end to the bigotry. I want everyone treated equal no matter who the are. And I especially want a special program to teach male deputies how to treat females, and females to learn how to not be over sensitive to stupid males who make stupid, but innocent mistakes. After that, decent training wherever training is required."

"It'll be fun handing them those demands. Especially the ones that cost money. You know how they whine about the budget." "Well, they can stick their budget straight up their ass. If they cut the graft, there'll be plenty left in the budget to give the department what it needs."

Before the day was over, Dale got a second call from a commissioner. "We still want a meeting," he said, "and we'll agree to everyone attending. Everyone, that is, other than Lisa Thomas."

Dale was quick to answer. "Everyone will be included in the meeting. Especially Lisa. You can't agree to that, instead of bothering me with your stupid, childish bullshit, you can go fuck yourself." He hung up.

Because it took half the commissioners on the board the rest of the day and half the next day to reconcile with the fact that there are some women on earth who have value beyond something to fuck, it was another late afternoon before Dale got his next call.

"I hope," Dale said when he answered the call, "you fucking morons have got your shit together, because if you haven't, this is your last chance. And if it is the last call, we have plans for something that will make everyone of you miserable for a very long time."

"We've agreed to allow all of you to attend the meeting. That should satisfy you."

"You can stick that bullshit up your ass." Dale was angry again. "You will *allow* all of us to attend the meeting. *Allow us?* You certainly are an ignorant piece of shit. The truth is, we will be the ones to allow such a meeting in the first place. So you and the rest of the dumb fucks on the board better improve your attitudes, or that meeting will be over before it starts. I hope even your shallow brain can understand that."

"I don't think you realize who you are dealing with on this issue, Dale. We are definitely not used to, nor are we willing, to put up with your kind of insubordination. We run this county, not you."

"Not for long, so again, go fuck yourself."

Dale called Mack. Mack put his cell phone on speaker so Lisa could take part in the conversation. Between them, they decided to start their lawyers working on all the paperwork required to start a private detective company.

Because they could afford them, they all had excellent lawyers, and the company was formed very quickly. While that was being done, it was at least part of the morning breakfast conversation whenever Lisa and Mack were there. And they were there nearly every morning.

It was a few days after they left the sheriff's office that Roy spoke up about what they were doing. "Are you two sure you're doing what you really want? You both loved working as sheriff's deputies. Be my guess that by now you can force the county board to let Lisa go back to work, if the rest of you do."

Mack answered. "I know we could. The key word though, is force. As long as they can't recognize and admit to the fact that they were completely wrong, we can't deal with them. And we'll actually be a lot freer as private detectives to do something about all the problems around here, than what we ever were as deputy sheriffs."

"And as for what I want," Lisa added, "I'll never get it from any of those creatures on the county board."

"Well, what is it that you want, Lisa?"

"Just the respect I earned for who and what I am. From them, what I get is nothing but putdowns. So for me, given their attitude, the move we're making is the right move."

Roy's face broke into a big smile. "I couldn't agree with you more, Lisa. The way those miserable excuses for humans are, the way they treat people, especially woman, is inexcusable. And I think you guys have a good idea, opening up your own private detective agency. I envy you, being able to do the things you're going to be able to do."

Roy's wife, Wanda, frowned at his comments. "Now don't be getting any ideas," she said to him. "You are too far up there in your years, to be playing detective."

Mack couldn't help himself then. He knew what a vigorous man Roy still was, and knew that he had a natural talent for the kind of work they'd be doing. "I don't want to argue with you, Wanda," he said. "But you're wrong about Roy. He's plenty young enough to do the work of a detective. And given what he does around here every day, he obviously has the energy."

"That might be true," she argued, "But if he did that full time, you all would expect me to manage this place alone. But even if I could, which I doubt, I damn sure don't want to."

Mack was starting on a roll now. "You won't have too," he explained.

"Well, who the hell's going to do it then?"

"No one. Not only Roy would make a good private detective, so would you. And you and Roy as partners would be great."

"You still haven't answered my question. Who's going to manage this place if I'm working with Roy?"

"Again, no one. Let's sell off all the cattle and any other animals Theresa doesn't want to take care of. We don't need the money from that business, and it does tie you guys down."

Ben interrupted them. "There's over four hundred acres here, Mack," he said, "You get rid of the cattle, what are you going to do with all that land?"

"To start with, let you use as much as you want for whatever you want to use it for. Then let the rest of it go back to nature. If nothing else, it will be fun to watch the changes, and how fast they happen."

This time Sue Sartor was the one to interrupt. "If you guys are going to do this, you'll need someone to deal with the technical work. Since I'm the one who has the experience in that department, are you interested in hiring me?"

Mack first answered with a smile. He followed that with, "That was going to be my next question. How would you like to be a partner in our new company?"

"There's nothing in this world I'd rather be."

Lisa said then, "That settles the issue. I'm delighted to have you a partner in the company, Sue. I think having you will make the difference between success and failure."

They all fully agreed with her.

Chapter 17

Even though the company (which they named Refuge Rescuers) wasn't ready to open yet, Mack and Lisa decided to start doing some investigating anyway. Since Mack's biggest concern was the environment, they checked out the latest developments in the river and refuge pollution.

It didn't take long to see that the problem was worse, and given what was going on up stream, it was only going to continue. After finding what they did, they decided to follow the river trail farther upstream to gather more evidence against the many hunting and fishing resorts located on the river.

When they came to the new, eight foot high, chain link fence across the trail, Mack lost all patience. The fence was on state land, and the people who built it there had no right, legal or otherwise, to do it.

He went home, loaded a Bobcat onto a trailer and drove it to the refuge. He unloaded it in the parking lot, then drove it through the refuge on the trail to the fence. He did some minor damage along the trail, but knew it would quickly heal.

He then used the Bobcat to tear down the fence. Once it was down he hauled it to his truck, loaded it, and took it to the Track And Trail Lodge. He unloaded it on the road outside the lodge, and hooked it behind the Bobcat in a way that would make it bounce and dig the ground to the maximum. He then proceeded to drag the fence along their newly paved driveway to their main barn. The driveway was new enough to still be soft, so the fence did a good job of tearing it up.

When a big, somewhat overweight man approached Mack with a face full of anger, Mack told him, "Not today. I've had enough of you people, so not today."

The man took a close look at Mack, shook his head yes, and walked away. Mack unhooked the fence, drove the Bobcat back to his truck, loaded it onto the trailer, and left for home.

"I thought for sure," Lisa, who was with him the whole time, said, "that guy was going to start a fight. What did you tell him that stopped him?"

"I told him I wasn't in the mood."

Lisa looked at Mack. There was nothing left for her to do. She laughed.

Shortly after they got home, Dale called again. Mack put his phone on speaker. Lisa stood next to him as they talked.

"The commissioners have called a press conference to explain how wrong we are. I think we should all be there for it."

"I couldn't agree more," Mack said. "I also think we should actually do whatever we can to be part of it. If we get lucky, we will be questioned too. It will give us a chance to counter some of their lies."

"You are right, Mack. It will be especially beneficial if they question Lisa. She always does an outstanding job dealing with those media people."

They agreed to meet at the site of the press conference fifteen minutes before it was scheduled to start. Dale contacted the deputies who were being forced to do crowd control at it, to let them know they were coming. It was a wise thing on Dale's part to do, because the commissioners had given the deputies explicit instructions to not allow Dale, Mack, or Lisa any where near it.

Since the deputies liked and respected those three, and hated the commissioners, they totally ignored those instructions. They even allowed them to stand at the back of the stage before the questions started.

The conference didn't start with questions, however. The commissioner's director insisted on reading a statement about Lisa's unfair suspension. He, of course, called it more than fair, and also said that it was for the safety of the community, since Lisa was so violent. He continued along that line, but his presentation was slow, tedious, and exceedingly boring.

Several of the reporters began looking closer at who was on the stage with the commissioners, especially in the back. They quickly noticed Dale, Mack, and Lisa. One of the reporters, who hated being forced to attend this kind of political stage for lies, stood up.

"I'd like to get the opinion of the people you are condemning," he said, interrupting the director.

"They're not here," the commissioner answered.

"Actually they are," the reporter told him. "They are standing right behind you."

Shocked, the man quickly turned his head. As soon as he saw them, he motioned for a deputy to come closer. "Get rid of them, right now," he said quietly, with his hand covering the microphone in front of him.

She smiled at him, shook her head yes, then walked away in the opposite direction of the three press conference invaders. The director slammed his fist down on the lectern and turned to the reporter.

"This press conference was called to explain why a very bad deputy sheriff was given a suspension. Its purpose is not to allow that woman to stand up here and lie."

A different reporter, a woman this time, stood up. "How do we know she's lying?" she asked, "if she isn't allowed to talk?"

"Because she's a proven lier. That's part of the reason she received such a long suspension."

"If she was such a proven lier, why would the sheriff and several other members of the sheriff's office quit in her support? Are you afraid to let her speak?"

"Of course I'm not afraid to let her speak. It's just simply not appropriate at this time."

A third reporter stood up. "Since when is looking for the truth not appropriate at a news conference? I think it's time to let Lisa Thomas defend herself against your accusations. The more you abject to her answering questions, the more it is that you look like the lier."

Lisa was smart enough to know that now was the time to answer questions. She moved to the lectern, and pushing her head close to the microphone, said, "I'm ready to answer any questions you might have."

The director was totally frustrated now, and made a big mistake. He pushed Lisa out of the way. She let him, then exaggerated the strength of his push. she staggered back, then fell and landed on her backside. Before she managed to get up, Dale picked up on what she was doing. Suppressing a smile, he rushed to the lectern.

"That," he said, pointing to Lisa, "is a perfect example of the bullying tactics of this group of commissioners. That's the kind of thing which has been going on too long. That's the kind of thing that made me quit in protest. And that's the reason that Lisa should be allowed to talk and answer questions now."

There was universal agreement among the reporters, that Lisa should be the one to speak now. None of them were interested any longer in what the director or any of the commissioners had to say. So Lisa took command of the lectern.

She answered each and every question with clear, concise, and honest answers. In doing so, she also told her own story, and even managed to get across the fact that had the suspension been reasonable, even though it was grossly unfair, would have been accepted. She also explained how and why the suspension they gave her was grossly unfair.

She was the one attacked, and now she was being punished for defending herself. She went on to explain that when attempts were made to reconcile the differences with the commissioners, they were so grossly insulting that now there was no chance of it happening. And finally, she told them that they were going to open a private detective agency.

"And the first order of business for the agency will be to investigate each and every commissioner, in order to protect the rights of all members of the sheriff's department from anymore of the county boards, if not illegal, immoral treatment of those people." She paused a moment, looking around to be sure she had the reporters full attention. "Also, because of the constant budget problems which has plagued the sheriff's department for many years, the new agency fully intended to check all of the commissioners activities, financial and otherwise, to ensure that they weren't involved in any kind of graft."

Lisa hadn't made any kind of direct accusations toward the commissioners, but she did let her tone of voice do it.

The one reporter who made it a habit to be nasty to any member of the sheriff's department whenever he got the chance, asked, "What else you people plan on doing in your agency, other than taking dirty pictures for people wanting a divorce."

Trying not to let her contempt for the reporter show, Lisa calmly answered, "We won't be participating in that part of the business. There's too much other work to do."

"Really now," the reporter sneered, "you people think you're too special to do that kind of work. You must know you'll never stay in business that way. It's the mainstay of your industry. Mark my words, it won't be but a few weeks before you're back here, whining to get your jobs back."

Lisa was about to answer him, when a shot rang out. The bullet hit the lectern, no more than an inch below the spot Lisa's hand rested on it.

Mack, who was now standing next to her, tackled her. Two more shots were fired in quick succession as they fell to the floor. One of the bullets hit one of the commissioners, still sitting behind the lectern. Lisa got to her feet and went to him, working frantically to stem the flow of blood from his wound.

Dale and Paul, who were not in the immediate line of fire, managed to spot the shooter. he was located on the top of a two story building, and the hunting rifle with a scope slowed him down considerably when he tried to climb off the building using the fire escape.

He reached the ground at the same time Dale and Paul reached the alley he was in. Paul yelled for him to stop, but as a typically stupid person is almost always likely to do, he quickly raised his gun and fired. He only got off the one shot before both Paul and Dale returned fire. They each shot twice. All four bullets hit him. Any of their bullets would have been enough to kill him.

The first thing Dale said when they walked up to the body was, "I damn sure am glad he wasn't using an AR15. If he had been, likely as not he could have fired fast enough to kill Lisa. He'd have gotten off that roof faster too. That rifle he was carrying was pretty bulky. The damn fool didn't even have a sling on it."

"All that's true. But why was he shooting at her. There's been an awful lot of people coming after her lately. I think that we'd best make figuring that out our first priority. We let anything happen to her, and none of what else we do makes any sense at all."

By the time they managed to get back to Lisa and Mack, most of the reporters, the commissioners, including the one who was wounded, were gone. The female reporter who took Lisa's side early during the press conference was talking to Lisa.

"I think," Mack told them, "that this incident happening where and the way that it did, is going to make Lisa look a lot better to people. She's responsible for that commissioner surviving. His wound wasn't so bad, but he would have bled out if she wouldn't have been there to stop the bleeding."

"That took a lot of guts on her part to go to him the way she did. She left herself wide-open to the shooter."

"She did," Mack agreed. "But speaking of him, the shooter I mean, did he make it?"

"No. He fired at us. We returned it. He missed. We didn't."

"That's too bad. I was hoping we'd get the chance to ask him why he was shooting at her. Did he have any ID on him?"

"He did. It was his own, real ID. His billfold had all the normal stuff a person would have in it. He lived in a place called Green Valley. I guess it's one of those retirement communities. It's south of Tucson."

"Well, That's a start anyway. Now all we have to do is figure out why someone in that part of the world wants her dead."

Chapter 18

The press conference the commissioners so badly wanted, would have normally gotten a fair amount of media coverage, especially given the way Lisa, Mack, and Dale managed to take it over.

Instead, it was the lead story throughout the media for an entire day. The shooting grabbed the attention of TV news show producers, and most of the print medium. Radio stations even played patriotic songs honoring what they called 'that brave little girl' from Kingsburg, Minnesota.

Everyone involved with Refuge Rescuers knew how much guts it took for Lisa to do what she did, yet at the same time they considered calling her that brave little girl was beyond simply stupid.

Initially, all the excessive publicity was annoying, but when inquiries about their new business started to come in because of it, it was no longer an irritation. It was an obvious asset.

They all took their share of calls and answered the questions prospective customers had. Mack though, was the one to catch the most interesting call. It proved to not only be an interesting job on its own. It also tied in with his investigations of the pollution being caused by the polluting hunting lodges located along the St. Catherine River. Pollution that was now having a serious negative impact on the wildlife refuge.

The person who contacted him was the sister of Jeffry Carro, the man who was shot by a gun salesman, while doing his job at the Track And Trail Resort. She introduced herself as Leslie Carro, and she had a most interesting case for them. Mack, Lisa, Dale, and Paul all became interested in his death from the time he was first reported missing.

The case became even more interesting when the man's body was found in a lonely pasture way the hell up in Canada. And not only found there, but dropped there from a plane by someone awful anxious to hide the body. The woman, who was so anxious to talk to someone about her bother's death, that she came directly to the Refuge Rescuers office rather than call.

Mack's first question for her was, "What can we do for you?"

"I want you to find out what actually happened to my brother." From there she went on to identify herself, then tell him about her brother. She ended her story with, "Do you think there's any chance you can find out for me."

Mack knew there was a lot of ways he could answer her, and that most of them would increase his chances of landing the job. A job he very much wanted. Instead, he decided to tell her the truth.

"To start with," he explained, "I really want the job. Solving that mystery will probably be as much to my advantage as it is to you. I've already been thinking about it, but just haven't been able to put much effort in it yet. Now I, we actually, if you give us the case, will all be looking into it. We now have the time. Even so, the chances of us finding a complete solution are slim."

He paused a moment before continuing. "As far as anyone working on the case can tell, whoever is responsible covered their tracks pretty well. It has also been a while since it happened, so all the evidence is cold. That means that now you have to decide, given the circumstances, is it worth it to you to hire us."

"I don't know," she said. "I guess that depends on how much you are going to charge me."

Mack quoted her what would be their normal rate. The numbers immediately set her back. It was easy to see that it was way beyond her budget.

"The thing is," he added, "because it is the case that it is, we will do it for expenses only. Even that can run into a fair amount of money, but no where near our normal fees."

"I definitely want to do it, but you have to keep me informed on the costs. When I reach my limit, I'll have to ask you to stop the investigation."

"I will definitely do that. Do we have a deal then."

"We do."

Since the people who were now part of Refuge Rescuers decided to make Ben and Theresa's their official meeting place every morning, Mack decided to wait until then to tell everyone about the new client.

Before he could do that though, each member of their group personally thanked Ben and Theresa for providing not only a place to meet, but also a delicious breakfast to go with it.

They all wanted to pay them for the service, but were soundly turned down for the offer. "I know," Ben explained, "that it will be a long time, if you ever do, before you'll show any kind of profit. I also know every one of you pretty well, so I know how much work you'll be doing free of charge. Because I do, and because I admire the fact that you are all so willing to help people out, this is the least I can do."

All of them knew Ben real well too, so they didn't argue with him. He was every bit as determined to do the right thing as they were. This home, this daily breakfast, would be their main meeting place for those who could make it, every day.

It was Mack's plan to make his new client the first topic of discussion. Dale surprised all of them when he spoke up first. "To start with," he explained, "I want all of you to know that I think what you're doing is great. The kind of agency you've formed is something very much needed right now."

Mack interrupted him. "From the tone of your voice, Dale, it sounds like you're not going to be part of it. Are you quitting us already?"

"No. I am definitely not quitting you. I am just going to be working with you in a different capacity than originally planned."

"How are you going to do that?"

"By taking the sheriff's job back."

"But how will...?"

"Just hear me out, Mack. If I don't take the job back, god only knows what we'll have to put up with in that job. For this operation to function properly, and the way we all want it to, we'll need to have someone in that office who will support what we do when we need and deserve support. I'm the best person there is to perform that function."

"Are you sure though," Mack asked, "that you want to return to that position, and have to deal with all those miserable commissioners?"

"Returning to the job is something I actually want to do. I loved it. Dealing with the commissioners, no. But this time will be different. Given all the really bad publicity the commissioners have gotten since the press conference, they are going to have to take me back under my terms. And, Mack," he said pointing at him, "all of that list you gave me will be on my list of demands. I damn sure plan to keep them on their toes."

"I can't tell you, Dale, how much I'll miss working with you on a daily basis. And tempted as I am to try to talk you into sticking around, I know you are right. Having you as sheriff will prove to be about as big an asset as we have."

Mack paused and looked around at everyone sitting at that large dining room table. Their eyes all held varied degrees pf sadness over Dale's leaving them. At the same time, they were all shaking their heads yes in agreement to his decision to go back to the sheriff's office. It didn't take a lot of thought to know that it would be a lot better to have Dale in that job, rather than someone who tried to block them every step of the way.

Seeing how everyone responded to his proposal, Dale stood up to leave them. Mack stopped him. "Stick around," he said. "I don't think you should leave us until you finish your negotiations with the board and have your job back."

"I know, but I thought that since I'm no longer a part of this agency, I shouldn't be part of your private business."

"Nonsense," Mack argued. "One way or the other, you'll likely be part of most of what we do, even if you aren't officially connected."

Dale shook his head in agreement and sat back down. Mack then brought up the subject of his new client. After he explained all that was connected with the case, he asked for questions.

Roy was the first to speak up. "Do you have a plan yet, Mack, on how you're going to approach the investigation?"

"I do, and I'm hoping you like it, because you and Wanda will both be involved, if you have no objections?"

"Why would I object? That's what we're here for, isn't it?"

"Yes and no. There will be some danger in what I have in mind for you, so if you think it's too much danger for either one of you, you guys have the option of bowing out of it."

Wanda spoke up. "I agree with Roy," she said. "Doing the job is what we are here for. If we were going to back out of any of what we need to do, then auctioning off the cattle a few days ago doesn't make any sense at all."

Mack's smile told them that he liked their response. "What I want you two to do is go undercover."

"How and where?" Roy asked.

"As guests at the Track And Trail Resort and Lodge where Jeffry Carro was working just before he disappeared. There's something about that place, and the people who own and manage it, that has me wondering about it. I don't have any idea how, but I have a gut feeling that they had something to do with his murder."

"That sounds serious. Do you think there's a chance they'll go after us?"

"I have no idea, Roy. But that's where the danger comes in."

"Doesn't matter, Mack," Wanda interrupted. "There's two of us. We'll be sure to watch each other's backs."

"I know that. But I still want you to go into it with as much knowledge as I can give you, to keep you safe as I can."

From there, they went over everything that would be needed to be done to get them ready for their undercover work. Sue Sartor was a big part of that process. She created both an online background for them, just in case someone might check that. She also created an extensive group of IDs for them. And finally, she managed to get legitimate credit card accounts using their new, but fake, IDs.

While she was doing that, and setting up their week long reservations for their stay at Track and Trail, Dale began his campaign to go back to work as the sheriff of Clayborne County. By then, the department was in such a shambles that it didn't take much to convince all of the commissioners that it would be a good idea to take Dale back. And they did it while accepting all of his demands.

He not only got everything Mack had said he wanted, but also a few requests of his own. The biggest of those was his demand that he, not the board, make the monthly budget proposal. He knew he'd rarely get everything he asked for in a budget, but he knew that it was better to argue about what they wanted to cut, then about things never brought up in the first place.

As soon as he was reinstated as sheriff, he set up special patrols to drive by Track And Trail on a regular basis while Roy and Wanda were guests there.

Chapter 19

Sunday morning, the day before Roy and Wanda were scheduled to start their week long stay at Track And Trail, Joseph Bakker gave a guest sermon at one of the local evangelical churches in the Lands Magnificent Resort complex. He was the father of Todd Baker, the man Lisa shot while they were in Tucson.

He began his sermon by praising God for so generously providing the United States Of America with such an awesomely great man as Donald Trump. He followed that with a warning about how the jews, blacks, queers, and especially Mexicans, were absolutely destroying the country.

From there, he got more specific. "We have an extra evil bunch amidst us at all times. Of all the evil ones, they are the ones most hated by God himself. The whores. The ones who pollute man's soul itself. There are too many to count and they are everywhere.

And here, in this very county, you have two of the worst who have ever existed since the beginning of time. One of them tried to destroy my son's moral soul when he was only a young boy. The other murdered my son. Those women should, no, *must* be removed from the face of the earth. Their names are Theresa Thomas and Lisa Thomas. All that is needed is men with the courage and enough faith in God to do so.

As great and good a man as Donald Trump is, he is still only one man. So we must follow his inspired by God guidance, and do our best to rid our society of the evil surrounding us. In doing so, we must all remember that God's law is the only law. Man's law, in comparison, means nothing. Therefore, you must rid us of the presence of those two evil women. By whatever means are necessary to do it.

And last, thank you for listening to my truth so attentively. May God bless you, America, and most especially, Donald Trump."

As soon as he left the pulpit he left the church. From there it was a fast ride to the airport where he boarded his private, rented, jet plane. It flew him back to the Tucson airport, where he got into a limo for his ride to his home.

Back at the church Joseph had so quickly deserted, a small group of men were discussing the various ways to do what the guest preacher had told them they should do. They took the task at hand very seriously. They might not have, had it only been the words of the preacher. But it was the words of the great and powerful Donald that convinced them. After all, he did constantly lecture about all the evil liberal people in society. And it was a fact that he did treat women as though they had little to no value. That led to the only logical conclusion. Donald Trump and the preacher, Joseph Baker wanted Theresa and Lisa Thomas dead. So dead is what they should be.

The evangelical men only had one problem when they planned how they would kill the two now hated women. They were exceedingly stupid. They decided that the simplest way to accomplish what was now their holy quest, was to drive to their homes, search them out, and shoot them.

So five of them got into an SUV, drove to the Thomases farm, got out of their vehicle, armed themselves, and split up to find the fallen women. They were closest to Ben's, so he saw them first. He called Mack, and Theresa called Roy, then followed with a call to Sue. Ben called 911 after Mack.

All three of the Thomas men, along with Lisa and Wanda, went on the hunt then. They weren't about to wait until someone got behind them and put a bullet in their back. At the same time, the would be women killers were wondering, almost aimlessly, around the houses. Ben came up behind two of them.

"Be a good idea," he told them, "to drop your weapons and lay yourself down in the dirt. I'm carrying a twelve gauge pump, and if I have to pull the trigger even once, that will be the end of the both of you.'

One of the men swung around and pulled the trigger on the rifle in his hands. He had a small problem though. He forgot to unlock the safety on the gun, so of course it didn't fire. Instead of shooting him, Ben took a couple of quick steps, then smashed the butt of his shotgun hard into the man's face. He was out before he finished falling. The second man dropped his rifle and meekly laid down on the ground.

Mack wasn't so lucky, and he was forced to shoot and kill the man he encountered. Lisa was luckier, and only wounded the one she went after. The one Wanda and Roy had to deal with was the most stupid of all of them. Even though he'd just seen a picture of Theresa, when he got behind Wanda, he yelled, "Okay, Theresa you whore, you are dead now."

He didn't get his gun to his shoulder. Roy shot him in the head, killing him instantly.

It all happened so fast that Mack got a chance to question the meek one who laid down on his own before the sheriff's department arrived. The man told him everything he wanted to know. When he was finished questioning the man, he turned to Lisa and said, "Looks like we're making another trip to Tucson. We can't let that preacher continue to send men here to kill you."

"I agree, Mack. If for no other reason than I'm damn sick and tired of it."

Dale was one of the first from the sheriff's department to get there after the shooting, so the investigation that followed was fair and accurate. It was obvious that this was another attack, and that none of the Thomases were guilty of any crime. Mack quickly saw the wisdom of Dale's move back into the sheriff's office. Without Dale running things, he could easily see how the commissioners might try to use this incident against him and his entire family.

Several members of the church confessed to the deputies who checked on the story about the sermon that it was in fact, real. The only repercussions to that was having the church shut down. Rodney Twilabee, the CEO of the Lands Magnificent Resort canceled the lease they had, and turned the building over to a group of Lutherans looking for a place for their Sunday services.

Roy and Wanda were a bit shaken by the attack, but decided to make their scheduled stay at Track And Trail anyway.

Chapter 20

Roy and Wanda arrived at Track And Trail as scheduled on Monday morning. As soon as they were checked in, the person at the desk told them that they were invited to a free luncheon at noon. It was sponsored by the Life's Protection Corporation, and they would be showing some of their latest weapons. They were told that if they found any of them interesting, the guns would be further demonstrated after the luncheon. They might even be able to try out one or two of them. It was highly recommended that they attend the lunch.

Neither Roy nor Wanda had any interest in listening to gun salesmen, but since they needed to start their investigation somewhere, it was as good a place as any.

When they got there, it was obvious the target audience was men. Only two women, other than Wanda, in attendance. Their dress, and the fact they were there alone, said their purpose there had little to do with guns. The dining area was already close to full, so they were forced to take a table close to the center of it. They would have much preferred a table nearer the back, where they didn't feel quite so exposed. As it turned out though, being somewhat exposed proved to be helpful, rather than detrimental to their investigation.

The food they were served was actually better than average for a place like that. It was breaded walleye, fried to perfection. The sides were french fries, browned to just the right crispness, and salad made from romaine rather than iceberg lettuce.

Even the gun presentations were less boring than Roy had expected them to be, so the meal time passed by quickly. When the gun salesmen invited those interested to join them at the rifle range, Roy was hesitant.

"I'd like to check it out," Wanda told him, a mischievous grin on her face. "It'll be fun to see what those hot shot guns can do."

One look at her and Roy knew what she was up to. She was an excellent shot, and always scored expert with any rifle in any contest she'd ever been in. She was one of those rare people who just didn't miss. When she pointed a gun at something, then pulled the trigger, the bullet landed exactly where she wanted it to.

She knew what kind of group she was in too. There was no doubt in her mind that they would object to her firing any of the guns. This was a place for men. Women did not at all belong. They were, after all, too frail and feeble to partake in this, a definite man's activity.

Roy only thought about it for a moment, then decided what the hell. Let her have her fun. He knew she could probably out shoot anyone else in the group. Even the salesmen, who were often expert shots. But even if she wasn't the very best, he knew she would come in real close to it.

At the range, the salesman demonstrated several of the rifles. They were all expensive, and for this demonstration they were all equipped with scopes to insure their accuracy. A half dozen men tested the rifles next, and all of them did a respectable job on the targets. That's when Wanda asked to test one of the rifles.

"I think," the salesman answered, "that all of these guns are a bit too much for a little lady like you. So why would you want to embarrass yourself in front of all these men here?"

Wanda knew this game real well. It was one she nearly always had to play at a time like this. "I'll tell you what," she told him, making sure she had a full smile on her face, and that she spoke loud enough for everyone to hear her, "I've got a hundred dollar bill in my pocket that says I won't. If I can't shoot at least as well as the rest of these gentlemen who already tested the rifles, I'll call you the winner."

The challenge proved to be too much for the man. "Okay," he said, "but I think it'll be only fair if you try out the lowest caliber rifle. I know damn well some of these guns are way more than you can handle."

Wanda laughed, then said, "Fine by me. But is it okay if I make my first shot a test of the scope. I generally do better when the scope is set right on."

The salesman only shook his head at her request. What the hell could she possibly know about scopes. But he let her have her way. "Fine by me," he agreed.

She surprised everyone when it only took her a moment to fire after lifting the rifle to her shoulder. When they checked her target, they found the bullet she fired slightly to the right of the center circle.

"Well," the salesman said, "it's obvious that the scope is dead on."

"No," Wanda told him. It's off to the right just a might." Before anyone could object, she made a slight adjustment to the scope. "That ought to do it." She lifted the semi automatic rifle to her shoulder, took just a moment to aim, then emptied the six shot magazine in rapid fire into the target.

All of her shots were grouped nicely in the center circle. She gave the salesman her biggest and best smile. He just stared back at her with his mouth hanging open.

"Well," she said, "I'll give you a choice now. You can either cough up the hundred, or you can let me test five more of the rifles of my choice. You do, and we can forget the bet."

"The thing is," he argued, "a bets a bet. I think I'll have to honor ours." He took out his wallet, found a hundred dollar bill, and gave it to her. "Now that we're even on that one," he challenged her, "how about we bet five hundred this time, that you can't do that five more times with five different guns."

"Sounds good to me, so long as I get that first shot with each gun to test the scope."

"I know they're all accurate, but I guess letting you test them is fair enough. I want something in return though."

Wanda didn't like the sound of that. "And what do you want?"

The salesman smiled now. He liked it that she'd misunderstood him. "Not that I wouldn't enjoy it," he said, "but definitely not what you're thinking. I want to be the one to pick out the guns you'll be firing."

"That I can go along with." She smile again. "So let's do it."

The first gun was more powerful than the one she used for the original bet, but not any serious kind of challenge for her. The scope proved to be dead on, but she took more time and care as she filled the middle circle on the target.

As she did the same with the next three guns, she continued to be increasingly more cautious when she took each shot. Everyone on the crowd was sure she was getting real nervous by then, so when the salesman gave her the heaviest and most powerful rifle there, a lot of the crowd was sure she would fail this time. A few people even made side bets against her.

She took extreme care when she made her test shot. Even she breathed a sigh of relief when the scope proved to be accurate. It was a tense group as she readied herself for the last go around. she moved her feet back and forth, then twitched her shoulders. There was no doubt in anyone's mind then, that Wanda was about as nervous and maybe even a bit scared. Five hundred dollars was on the line and here she was with a gun way to big for her that she'd only fired once in her life.

Very slowly she raised the rifle to her shoulder. Taking more time than what should have been necessary, she took careful aim. Then she shocked everyone. Even to some extent, Roy. She pulled the trigger on the big, over powered gun as fast as she could move her finger. They were all sure then, that her nervousness had done her in.

But when the dust settled, they found that it would have been close to impossible for her to have made a tighter patter in the middle of the target's middle circle.

When the salesman tried to pay the bet, she waved him off. "It wasn't a fair contest," she said. "I knew before this started, what I could do. You had no way of knowing. Besides, you gave me what I really wanted. The chance to test some of your guns. So please, just consider the whole thing even."

"I'm not really all in favor of settling it this way, but I will go along with it on one condition."

A once more suspicious Wanda asked, "And what condition is that?"

Once again the salesman smiled at her reaction to him. "Again," he said, "not that. I'd just like to buy you and your husband a drink. I think that's the least I can do."

Wanda waved Roy over to them. "Ask him," she told the salesman.

Before he asked Roy about the drink, he finally introduced himself. He stuck out his hand to Roy. "Gunther Johnson," he said.

Roy gave him the names they were currently using, and then agreed to having the drink. The three of them went to the bar in the club house. They sat in at a small table, with Roy and Wanda on one side and the salesman on the other. Roy made no effort to take their conversation into anything even remotely connected to their investigation. It was too soon.

Gunther started the conversation anyway. "Do you know," he asked, "that your wife refused to take the money she won?"

"I figured she would. We knew that there was no way she'd lose the bet, even before it was made."

"She's that good?"

"She is. Has been since she was a kid."

"And sometimes," she said with a smile, "I like to show off some. That's part of what I was doing with you. Doing it to someone like you, who's in the gun business and knows how to use them, is especially fun. And in the end, you guys are the ones who know what it takes to be able to do what I can do, so you are the ones most impressed by it."

"Oh, I was impressed. There's no doubt about that."

"That is as you should be," Roy said. "Being in the gun business, you know how rare she is. But people like her being rare or not, it'd be my guess that business is good for you guys now."

"I sure can't complain any. I only sell hunting and target guns, be they handguns, rifles, or shotguns. I'm very much a gun person, and I love shooting, but I can't say I think much of those assault rifles that are so popular now."

"I don't either. They were designed for killing people, and really aren't much good for anything else. Not to mention, anyone who needs one of them for hunting, shouldn't be allowed to hunt."

"That is true. I'm damn sure glad that for the most part, I don't have to deal with the people who want to own those guns. This job, good as it is most ways, offers enough problems on its own."

"Really? I thought it was probably pretty simple. Guns tend to sell themselves, don't they?"

"They do, but we still have to bring them to the public. Like most other things, very few will find them on their own. So the constant travel can get to a person."

Roy was beginning to think that his conversation with Gunther might produce something dealing with the investigation, so he tried to keep it going. "I can imagine," he said, "that could get tiring."

"It does," Gunther agreed, then sighed heavily. "And sometimes it can get to be a lot more than that. It killed one of our guys."

"What? Did he have a heart attack or something?"

"Nothing that simple or straight forward. He was here when the problem started. I think he was directly involved with whatever it was, but I'm not sure he was. Anyway, whatever the incident was, it was big enough, important enough, so the whole group here to settle a big wholesale deal was sent home."

"That couldn't have been all bad," Roy said. "Going home, I mean."

"For him, it was." Gunther shook his head, almost as if he wished he could rid himself of the memory. "The thing is, when he got home, he was two days early. He caught his wife in bed with his best friend."

"That's something that none of us ever want to happen."

"For sure. It really set him off. Way beyond how I would ever have thought he'd react. I think there must have been something else bothering him, for him to do what he did. He just wasn't that kind of guy."

"He must have done something real radical then." Roy was now finding this story very interesting. "What was it?"

"I kind of hate talking about this. I almost wish I wouldn't have brought it up."

"I can understand that," Roy said, doing his best to sound sympathetic. "But gross as I might seem now, you sure have got me curious about what happened."

"And it is a curious thing. He took out a pistol, shot his wife and his friend, killing them both. Then, just as bad, he turned the gun on himself and put a bullet in his own head."

"Oh, that poor man," Wanda finally said. "It's terrible when that happens to anyone. He must have been depressed about something already, for him to react so strongly about something so simple as just sex."

The way she expressed herself about the sex part came across just innocent enough to change their somber mood. Both men broke into smiles. Gunther wondered about her comment, after the way she reacted toward him when she thought he proposition her. It was a big contradiction.

Roy had his own comment to make. "I don't know, Darlin'" he said. "I don't think I'd exactly react in a kindly manner if I was to find you in that position."

"In the first place," she said, a big frown now on her face, "there's no damn way in hell you ever would. You are the only man I want, and the only man I will ever want. Even if you died and I was alone, there would never be another man. But I still don't think he needed to do all that killing."

"I think you're right," Gunther said, "about both things. After the way you reacted to me when you misunderstood what I was saying, not once, but twice, your loyalty to your man is surely true. And like you, I think it was way too much killing over sex. There must have been something else on his mind."

"It sure sounds like it," Roy said. "How long ago did all that happen?"

Gunther told Roy the approximate date. He added, "I'm just damn glad I wasn't one of the sales staff here when whatever it was happened. Some of the guys who were here, still seem to be somewhat bothered whenever the subject is brought up. None of them want to talk about it at all."

"That's strange," Wanda said. "Sometimes, when someone you know does something so horrible as suicide, it's better to talk about it."

"That's not the problem. The suicide's been plenty talked out. No, it's whatever happened here that everyone's avoiding."

"That does sound like a mystery," Roy said. "Think you'll ever figure it out?"

"I doubt it," Dereck said. "Mostly, I think I'll just try to forget it."

Six young men, all of them six feet or more tall and weighing over two hundred and fifty pounds, came into the bar. They wore sweat shirts with the name of an out of state college. Roy assumed that they were all part of a football team. They all obviously had too much to drink. They split up and four of them moved to the table of two pretty young ladies sitting alone a a small table.

The other two moved over to Wanda. From the look on their faces and the way that they moved, they made it clear that they considered

Roy and Gunther to be completely insignificant. One of the men put his hand on Wanda's shoulder and squeezed. She pushed it off. He put it back on.

"If you had any kind of a brain," she said, pushing the hand away again, "you'd walk away while you still can."

He didn't. He moved his hand back onto her and said, "You're too damn good looking to be wasted on these old men. It's time you found out what a real man is."

That was more than Wanda was willing to put up with or listen to. Quicker than the man with the wandering hand could think, let alone move, she was on her feet. Her strong hand reached between his legs, grabbed him and squeezed as hard as she could. He screamed and doubled over in pain. She stepped back, locked her hands together, and slammed them down on the back of his head.

Before he hit the floor, Roy was on his feet. The second man ignored him and took a swing at Wanda. She ducked out of it and he took the man out with a couple of hard blows to his gut and a solid right under his chin.

The other four men now rushed to the aid of their two friends laid out on the floor. Gunther was now standing next to Roy, and Wanda was on the other side. As the four men grew close, they suddenly stopped and stared. Roy and Gunther both carried big angry frowns on their faces and were obviously ready to fight. But that wasn't what stopped the men.

When they got close they all recognized Wanda from the earlier shooting match. More than that, the wide grin on her face, and the way she held her hands in front of her, waving her fingers for them to bring it on, scared the hell out of them.

She not only could shoot better than any man they'd ever seen, she'd just handily dispatched their friend with seemingly little effort. And now she was smiling at them to bring on the fight. It was too much. There was something utterly unreal about that woman. And the last thing they ever wanted to do was lose a fight with a woman. Something inside told them they probably would, so they meekly, without a word, picked up their friends and carried them out of the bar. They didn't return.

The two young ladies who were sitting alone left their table then and joined them. They were full of thanks for getting rid of the drunks, and also full of flirty. The prettiest of the two, who was definitely dressed to attract men, tried to move in on Roy.

Her moves didn't please Wanda in the least. She moved close enough to the woman so she could feel Wanda's breath when she talked. "Not this time, Honey," she told her. "It would definitely be to your benefit for you to back off my husband."

The woman looked at Wanda, thinking she could make her back down. She then saw the look in Wanda's eyes. It only took an instant to make her decide she didn't want to feel that much pain. She quickly turned to Gunther.

With two women now resting a hand on each shoulder, his face was filled with a smile. Roy and Wanda were happy for him, but were ready to go back to their cabin. If Roy thought he could get anything more out of Gunther, he would have wanted to stay, but now that the situation had changed, he knew that trying to learn more would best be left for another day.

They made their goodbyes, and held hands on the way back to their cabin. Once they got there, they didn't bother to talk. After the young lady made it so apparent that she was interested in Roy, it triggered something in Wanda. As soon as the cabin door closed behind them, she reached for the top button on his shirt.

Chapter 21

Mack was sitting on a chair, close to the one Sue was on. Her hands were working the keyboard of her computer, and her face was a study in concentration. Suddenly her expression changed, and she rapidly zipped through through several files on her computer screen.

"This is it," she said. "The police report about about finding the body in the pasture the Canadiens didn't want to release to us. Just because they consider us some kind of pariah now that we've gone private."

"Yeah, and they're not too fond of Dale either, since we're his ex-employees. They wouldn't give him much either."

"That's okay though." She smiled. "I've found all that I need to get into their files anytime we want to."

They took the time then to make note of all the dates, times, addresses, and other miscellaneous information they wanted. Sue then manipulated the files to make it near impossible for anyone to discover that she'd hacked that Canadien police departments file.

"We've got the information, Mack," she said, so what's the next step?"

"I think the best thing we can do is go to Canada and talk to the man who found the body. He doesn't own a phone, so going there is the only way we can talk to him. Then, depending on what we learn, it might be a good idea to visit the police department up there."

"Are you sure that isn't a waste of time? None of those people have been what you could call friendly."

"Actually, I think that at best we only have about a fifty fifty chance of learning anything. At the same time, I think we owe our client the best effort we can give her to solve this. That means we talk to the cops up there."

"You always give your best, no matter what. It just surprises me sometimes, the way all of you try to do the best you can with everything you do. It's a rare thing."

"Maybe. But you having that attitude has a lot to do with the fact that you don't just fit in with our family. It's why you are now part of it."

Sue blushed lightly from his compliment. "That's an awfully kind thing to say, Mack."

"No, it's only speaking the truth. And we're really lucky to have you."

"Not as lucky as I am to be here, and to be part of all this. But that's enough of that. Some of this is hard enough for me, Mack, without you being so damn nice to me."

Mack looked into her eyes and knew he better change the subject.

He wasn't the only one to realize he should change the subject. Roy had just asked one of the guides at Track And Trail about the mysterious goings on when Jeffry Carro disappeared and Doug Welch, the gun salesman, went home and shot himself.

Instead of any kind of answer, the guide glared hard at him, then turned his back on Roy. His non-answer, however, told Roy a lot. If his somewhat innocent question could bring on that much hostility, there had to be something serious to whatever happened.

He knew too, that he'd have to be very careful about what he said and did for the rest of his stay with Track And Trail. Given the fact the place was already involved in something serious, he knew from experience that they might be capable of nearly anything.

And they were. It just turned out to be something way different from the violence that all too often followed when someone stuck their nose into something someone was trying to hide.

Word quickly spread throughout the resort employees that care must be taken with any conversations with Roy and Wanda. It wasn't long before the owner of Track And Trail, Derrick James was told about Roy and Wanda's excessive curiosity about the shooting incident and the disappearance of Jeffry Carro.

The last thing he wanted at his resort was another killing. But he knew he had to do something about the curious couple. And he needed to get the job done before Carson Chamber's got involved. Given that so far they'd managed to control everything related to the shooting with a lot of generous bribes, he decided to see if he could get rid of Roy and Wanda with one more.

Because they seemed to be such an ordinary middle class couple, he was sure he could do it with what he considered was small change. Ten thousand dollars would have little to no impact on his net worth of over a billion, so that's what he took out of his safe and gave to his number one assistant.

"Find those people," he told the man, "and tell them they can keep the money, if they immediately vacate the premises. Make sure they understand that we very much want them gone."

He found Roy and Wanda at the deer pen, watching the deer feed. They had their backs to him when he approached them, so he grabbed Roy by the shoulder. Roy didn't hesitate, and instantly spun around and nearly took the man out. He somehow managed to stop his flying fist before it landed on the man's face.

"Hey, man, take it easy. I mean no harm. I just want to talk to you."

"So talk," Roy growled.

"There's no reason to get hostile," the man claimed. "I'm just here to offer you a deal I'm sure you won't want to pass up."

"I'm sure your life will be a longer one, if you're careful with whatever kind of shit it is that you're going to try to hand me."

"Well, yeah sure, but just calm down," the man stammered. He wasn't at all used to dealing with men who had Roy's temperament. He could also tell from the look in Roy's eyes, that he'd best tread lightly. There was no point in getting into a brutal fight just to deliver a bribe. He handed Roy the envelope filled with the ten thousand dollars in hundred dollar bills. "What's in there is yours. All you need to do is leave the lodge today. Right now. And agree to stay away."

Roy opened the envelope and flipped through the bills. He looked at the man. "Why?"

"Damned if I know. I'm only the messenger. All you got to do now is tell me yes or no."

Roy didn't have to give it much thought. He'd learned a lot, and had a pretty good idea of what happened the day the mystery began.

He knew too, that their time there was for the most part used up. So he looked the man in the eye and said, "Yes. We'll be out of here in about an hour. All we got to do is pack."

The man nodded and walked away.

Roy and Wanda walked slowly back to their cabin. He used his camera as they walked, to take pictures of anything and everything that looked at all like it might be a source of the river pollution.

They quickly packed, and didn't see anyone of note on their way out. As soon as they were a safe distance away from the place, Wanda called Dale and asked him to meet them at the sheriff's office. As they went in, someone drove slowly by, watching them.

As soon as they sat down in Dale's office, Roy gave him the envelope of money, and in detail told him what they'd learned while they were at the Track And Trail resort/lodge. Dale took meticulous notes, and also recorded Roy's statement. When they finished, Dale turned off the recorder.

He smiled at Roy. "You know, Roy," he told him, "you could have kept the money."

"No, Dale, I couldn't. To start with, if you're holding it, there's a good possibility it might turn out to be evidence one of these days. More than that though, to me, it's blood money. Something I don't need and wouldn't want even if I was dead broke. Which we're a long way from being."

"I can appreciate that. The world would be a better place if everyone had your honesty. So what's next for you guys?"

"The first thing we want to is just go home," Wanda answered. "I want to get in the shower and wash the stink of that place off me."

"I feel the same way," Roy agreed. "But for now, we need a ride. Someone driving by when we came in here was watching us. For now at least, I'd prefer that they don't find out who we really are and where we live."

"What about your truck out front? What are you going to do with it?"

"Just leave it there for now, Dale. It's not worth a whole lot, so I doubt anyone will try to steal it. You can move it around back later, and I'll come and get it late tonight."

After they got home, showered and took a short nap, they met with Mack, Lisa, Sue, and Paul at Ben and Theresa's. It was getting late in the afternoon then, so Ben put together a light supper for everyone.

Roy started out their conversation by explaining about their visit with Track And Trail. He was frequently interrupted by comments from Wanda. As soon as they'd mostly cover all that happened, Roy told Sue it was time to get rid of the people they were at the lodge. She promised to get online right after their meeting.

Mack and Sue then told everyone what they'd learned about the events in Canada. Mack finished with, "I think, given how resistant the Canadiens have gotten about sharing information with us, it would be a good idea for one or two of us to take a drive up there. Lisa and I will be going beck to Tucson in a couple of days, or we would go. Even if we can't get anything much from the cops up there, we might learn something from the guy who found the body. Larry Jameson was his name. I think that one of the cops up there said he was a bit of a recluse."

"I thought those cops weren't talking to us?" Roy asked.

"This was before they shut us down. They are now just barely talking to Dale. They want nothing to do with us because we're private cops now. They don't approve of what we did, or what we're doing now. They claim that all we care about is the big money we're making on everything that we do."

"If there's no one else," Roy said, "Wanda and I can go. If possible though, we'd like a day or two to rest after our visit at that wonderful, gun happy lodge."

"You can, but one day's better than two. The sooner we get things up there checked out the better."

Chapter 22

Carson Chambers was furious. "I can't believe how totally fucked up you are, Derrick. From where I sit, you can't do a damn thing right. First, you let that useless bastard Mack Thomas tear down that brand new fence you just installed. Then he destroys your new driveway when he drags your fence down it. What the hell is wrong with you. You didn't even have to do a damn thing more than get the law on him."

"I couldn't do that."

"And why the hell not?"

"The fence was illegal. It was built on public land."

"Then you should have made it legal. You've got enough money. Money can make anything legal, if you spend enough of it."

"That's not so simple here, Carson. Here, unlike where you live, we frequently are forced to put up with a lot of cops, too many judges, and even a lot of lawyers who are honest."

"What about those county commissioners? They're pretty much bought and paid for, aren't they?"

"They were, until that fiasco they created with the sheriff's department. Now, for them, it's pretty much all duck and cover. The media is constantly on their asses, so it'll be a while before they can do us much good."

"Well, we damn sure have to do something about all the shit going on there. What about that couple that was asking all the questions? What are you doing about them?"

"I gave them ten grand and sent them on their way. I don't think they'll be anymore trouble."

"You can't be sure of that." Carson was growing ever more angry. "You did have them thoroughly checked out, didn't you?"

"Well, yes, but…"

"But what. You'd best not be telling me that you don't know everything there is to know about them."

"That's what I'm telling you. They disappeared. I had them followed when they left here, but when they made a stop in Kingsburg, they never returned to their truck. They were all the sudden gone. We haven't been able to find a trace of them."

"Did you have someone get online to check them out?" Carson was once again wondering how Derrick ever got rich, stupid as he was.

"I did. There's nothing there. Every trace of them is gone. Even all the credit card info. And they used a legitimate card. But it's gone from all records now. It's like they never existed."

"Jesus H Christ man. Don't you have a brain left. Did you at least check out to see what they were doing at the building where they disappeared?"

"We couldn't do that."

"And why the hell not, Derrick. It couldn't have been that complicated."

"It was. They stopped at the sheriff's office."

"Man, you have made us one hell of a godforsaken mess. Is there even one thing you can tell me about either one of them. Anything at all that sets them apart from anyone else?"

"Just one thing. The woman. She was an expert shot. During the gun demonstration your salesman put on, she convinced him to let her try out one of the rifles. She ended up putting on quite a show of marksmanship. Everyone one here who watched her, claims they've never seen anything like it. Oh, and she said she liked your rifles. She said they were well made."

"That ain't much to go on, Derrick, but it's something. Get someone on it."

"On it how. Lot's of people know how to shoot. Where the hell do we start looking?"

"I frankly don't give a damn where you start. What I give a damn about is that you do something about all the damn problems you have there, that you don't seem to ever solve."

"All those problems aren't so damn easy to solve. I live in a place where I can't just buy my way out of every bit of trouble the way you always do. And even if I could, I don't have your kind of money."

"No, Derrick, I'm sure you don't. And if all this crap continues, you might end up losing what you have. You have to get your shit together, man, before I'm forced to do something drastic."

"What the hell do you mean by that, Carson?"

"Even a man as stupid as you frequently are, Derrick, should be able to figure that out. You better anyway, if you don't want me to carry this out as far as it could go." Carson hung up the phone.

Derrick sat at his desk for a while, holding his head up with his hands. His eyes were closed and he was breathing deeply, wondering why he constantly was forced to put up with the likes of Carson Chambers. Life would be so much better with that man dead and gone.

He continued to think about it as he unlocked and opened a lower drawer of his huge, solid white oak, roll top desk. Gently, almost as if was his child, he removed the highest caliber hand gun made. He loved the gun, even if it was made by Carson Chambers' company, Life's Protection Corporation. It didn't even matter that Carson gave him the gun during a rare moment when he wasn't angry about something.

Derrick lifted the gun, pointed it at the picture he hated of Carson Chambers hanging on the wall not far from him, and dreamed of pulling the trigger. "Someday," he thought, "someday I might just do it to the man himself. Be fun to see him try to buy away the bullet I'd put in his forehead."

Sighing heavily, he put the gun back into its special resting place, closed the drawer and locked it. Having gone through the pleasure of handling the gun, he leaned back in his chair, now hoping his secretary was in the right mood. Dealing with the gun aroused him, and he wanted to make use of his body's reaction during the short time it lasted.

Carson Chambers got the same effect from threatening Derrick. For him, it was a great turn on to abuse anyone he considered beneath himself. And that included all but a very few members of the human race. And like Derrick, he wanted to make use of his arousal while it lasted. So he hastily left his mansion, and walked to his daughters. He found her sunning herself on her private patio. She wasn't dressed, and her husband was sitting close by, watching her.

Carson ignored him, grabbed her hand and said, "We need to talk."

He led her to her bedroom, laid her down in the middle of the bed, undressed, and quickly found his release. She didn't move a muscle as he did.

"That could have been better," he complained as he dressed.

"I suppose," she more or less agreed with him. "But you're getting old, Dad. Slam bang just doesn't do it for me."

"Well, it better start. That is, if you want to keep the life style you have now."

"I better keep it," she threatened, "or I will make you regret it."

Carson reached over and slapped her face. "Careful what you say, Shanty," he said with a nasty smile. "I'm the one with the money and power. Even you can be taken care of, if I ever feel the need to."

He walked out of the bedroom. What he didn't see as he left was his son in law lift his finger, point it at the back of his head. and make a soft sound like a gunshot. He went into the bedroom.

"Gerald," Shanty said to him, "instead of beating on me this time, why don't you come her and finish what that miserable old bastard started."

He thought, "What the hell, why not?"

He was almost gently with her, but when she managed to actually climax, it made him furious. Her father had started it with her, and no matter the reason for her doing it, the result should never be any kind of pleasure on her part.

When he started to beat on her this time, he was unable to stop himself. He just continued to beat on her until her face was a bloody pulp. When he finally came to his senses, and realized what he'd done, it was too late to do anything about it.

Carson returned, wanting his daughter for a second time. When he walked in the room and saw her covered with blood, he quickly moved to the place where Shanty kept the gun he gave her when she just barely old enough to learn how to use it. He took it out and emptied it into Gerald's chest.

He called the police, who arrived in minutes. They were cautious to treat him with utmost respect. Their questions for him were minimal, and by the time Shanty reached the hospital, any case against Carson was pretty much a closed issue.

He knew that would be the case. No one was about to accuse him of any crime. Not with the kind of money he had. Besides, there was a lot of sympathy for Shanty. Sympathy that carried over to him.

For him, the sympathy he felt was only for himself. Now he was going to be forced to find someone to replace her. He knew that would be a difficult task. He'd used her for so long, that he'd grown to need her. How she felt about it all this time didn't matter to him. It was how he felt about it that mattered.

After thinking about it for a while, he decided that the mystery women who was so good with a gun might be a suitable one for a while. If she could be found. In the meantime, he'd have to get in touch with the right people.

Lisa Thomas would do nicely too. She was beautiful, feisty, and would put up a decent fight while he raped her. And rape her he would. Given the problems her and her husband Mack gave him, she deserved nothing less. Forcing Mack to watch would be good too. He would get a lot of satisfaction from watching Mack being forced to watch him work over Lisa.

Chapter 23

Because of the multiple attempts to attack Lisa, Mack was doubly guarded when they left for Tucson. He not only watched his mirrors for anything suspicious, he watched everything happening on the freeway, the rest stops, and the truck stops.

It was their first stop for fuel after going around DesMoines that he began to believe they were being followed. Two men got out of their SUV when they followed Mack and Lisa into the truck stop. That alone wasn't enough to raise Mack's suspicions a great deal. It was the way the man pumping the gas kept glancing over their way that did it.

Second to that, when he finished pumping the gas, he didn't immediately go inside the building. He waited until the other man, who did go inside the building right away, to return before he went in. To further check on the two men he called Lisa, who was inside the building, and told her to return to the truck as quick as she could.

She was back at the truck in a couple of more minutes. They left the truck spot right away. As they pulled onto the street, Mack saw the man who pumped the gas into the SUV run out of the truck stop's building and rush to get out of the truck stop and behind Mack and Lisa again.

It was all the proof Mack needed. They were being followed. Given their reasons for being on the freeway, heading for Tucson, Mack expected any trouble they would run into would be from the people in Tucson. Those two men now following them, he was sure, were not from Tucson. The people from there who had gone after Lisa, had always done it on the cheap. From the vehicles they drove, the weapons they used, and even the clothes they wore.

The men now following were driving a new, high end SUV. Even from a short distance away, their clothes appeared to be tailored and expensive. So who were? And why were they following them. He asked Lisa what she thought.

"I really don't have any great ideas, Mack," she said. "The only thing I can think of is that it might have something to do with the case Roy and Wanda are working on? Or maybe someone high up in the hunting lodge business doesn't like our snooping around and taking pictures."

"You could be right about that. And since the franchise business, Track And Trail, is owned by that guy who also pretty much owns that gun maker, Life's Protection Corporation, all of that could somehow be connected. The killing, the pollution, selling ever more guns, all of it. The trouble is, now I'm not worried about just us. Roy and Wanda might be in much the same kind of situation as we are. I know how smart and capable they both are, but they are nowhere near as experienced with this kind of thing as we are."

"Well," Lisa said, "now is a good time for me to use a piece of today's technology that so often drives you nuts. I'll call them on my cell phone."

Mack shook his head and laughed. "Good idea," he said. "Call them. And, I do get the message. I'll try not to bitch quite so much about them in the future."

Lisa called them and talked to Roy. Wanda was driving. They went over, in detail, what Roy and Wanda should watch for, what kind of men would be involved with any kind of attack, and all the reasons that it might happen to them. They ended the call with a big thank you for calling from Roy.

The SUV stayed way back from them for the next couple of hundred miles, but Mack and Lisa still knew it was there. Several times Mack considered trying to lose it, but decided to wait until after they drove the Kansas turnpike and were off the freeway before doing anything rash.

The SUV continued to keep its distance even after they moved onto the two lane highway, but by then the men in it were aware of the fact Mack and Lisa knew they were being followed. When they stopped for the night, the two men got a room in the same motel.

They even crossed paths as Mack and Lisa left the office. As they did, one of the men gave Lisa a lecherous look. It was enough to make Mack wish he could put a bullet in the man right there.

"Can't do that now," Mack thought to himself. "But if you two try anything with us later, we'll see. I'm really damn tired of all the violence around us, but with you two, I think I can make an exception."

Mack and Lisa slept in shifts that night, so they were still somewhat tired when they got up in the early morning. As they got ready to leave the motel, Lisa noticed a car parked in front of a room, two doors down. It was somewhere in the neighborhood of ten years old, but the body was free of rust. It carried Arizona plates She took the time to write down the license number, and as she did, she noticed a small bumper sticker. All that was on it was the name of Joseph Bakker's church in Tucson, along with a phone number. She pointed it out to Mack.

"You know," he said, "they could have been following us this whole time. We've been concentrating so damn hard on those other two, that we could have missed this one. Let's see what we can do about them."

He went into the tool box in the back of his truck. He took out a very sharp hunting knife with an eight inch blade. Then he proceeded to poke all four tires on both vehicles that had been following them. Then he knocked on the door of the room with the two men in it, while Lisa knocked on the other door.

They purposely took their time leaving the parking lot. When a total of five men came out of their rooms he waved at them. They all returned the wave with a shake of their fists.

"Do you think there's any chance they'll call the police on us for doing that?" Lisa asked. "We sure screwed them up."

"I seriously doubt it. If they had us arrested, it would mess up whatever their plans for us are. The men in the SUV obviously are bankrolled heavily, so they'll likely be able to get their tires repaired or replaced in a relatively short time. The other three will probably have a harder time of it. If they're getting paid for coming after us, I doubt that it's much. So they're going to be farther behind."

"What are you thinking then? That we can deal with them one bunch at a time this way."

"Not so much that. It's more that I want them really pissed off at us."

"What the hell for. Don't you think they're going to came at us hard enough without having them angry too?"

"The thing is, Lisa, you know as well as I do that no one thinks as clearly when they're good and pissed off as they otherwise might do. But more than that, now they know about each other. They're either going to work together, in which case we've got them bunched up so they come at us with one shot, or they'll be competing for a chance at us. They do that, and maybe we can figure out a way to use it against them."

"Have you to it figured out how to use it against them?"

"Not yet."

Lisa sighed. "Well, Mack, then you'd best let me drive so you can give it your all to figure it out. Otherwise, we are damn sure out numbered, and I don't think I'm going too much like the consequences of them winning this contest. I saw how that creepy bastard looked at me in that motel office. My gut says those two want the both of us for something beyond just killing."

They were for the most part quiet for the rest of the ride that morning. Lisa did nearly all the driving, and Mack went over all the various ways it might be possible to get the two groups of men at each other's throats if they hadn't joined forces. He then tried to come up with the best plan to set a trap for them if they were now working together. Nothing he came up with satisfied him.

He even considered driving to the Los Cruces airport, renting a private jet, and flying back home. They were on their way to Tucson in the hope they could stop the constant attacks on Lisa, but he couldn't help think that getting them both killed was a really poor way of stopping them. But that gave him an idea. He explained it to Lisa when they stopped for lunch at a truck stop too busy to be attacked in.

"Let's go to the Los Cruces airport, rent a private jet in our own names, and have it fly without us to Minnesota. We can then use our other IDs that Sue set us up with and rent a car. We'll have to let them catch up with us this afternoon though, so we make sure they think we actually did fly back to Minnesota. I think to start with, we'll only have to deal with the first two."

"What's your plan for doing that?"

"When they leave the airport, we follow them. At that point, there won't be anything for them to do, but try to find us back in Minnesota."

"Well, they might do what we did and fly back. We won't be able to deal with them then."

"No, but they will be out of our way then. They're the professionals, so they're the ones who might give us the most trouble. If, however, they do head back toward Minnesota the same way as we came down here, there's a lot of lonely highway in New Mexico. If we catch them off guard, it'll be a good spot as any to confront them."

"After we confront them, then what, Mack? You don't really think they'll back off do you?"

"I know that it'll be difficult to convince them to do it, but we have to try."

"Why don't we just let them drive away?"

"Because sooner or later, one way or the other, they'll figure out that we weren't on that plane. When they do, they'll be on their way back after us in Tucson. We don't confront them, then we should be on the plane, not here."

"That sure doesn't leave us with a hell of a lot of choices, does it Mack. Either we set them up with something that will likely end up in gun fight, or we give it up and go home."

"And either way, we've still got those other three fools to contend with. Not to mention what's ahead for us when we get to Tucson."

"I'll tell you what, Mack," Lisa complained, "I'm really damn sick and tired of this. All I want to do now is go back home and settle down to running our detective agency. I want to just take on cases where people need our help and we don't have to commit any violence to do it. But I know that first, we have to get through this crises. So let's set up the confrontation and hope for the best."

After lunch, they slowed their speed considerably, and about fifty miles out of Los Cruces the SUV caught up with them. Seeing it was actually a relief for Mack. Now they could start their plan. It wasn't perfect, he knew, but it would at least ultimately catch the two men in the SUV by surprise. And Mack hoped that would be enough to give him and Lisa enough of an edge to settle the problem in their favor.

While he settled the deal with the private airline for the rental of the small jet, Lisa checked to see what the two men from the SUV were doing. She found a new problem. It wasn't two men. It was five. The men hoping to either attack or at least grab her and Mack had joined forces. That now put the odds very much in their favor if there was a fight.

At the same time there was a big plus in their getting together. Joseph Bakker was one of the three men. Now, if she and Mack could somehow win this thing, it would also complete their mission to Tucson.

When Lisa told him what she saw, Mack had the same mixed feelings about it that Lisa had. Taking Joseph Bakker out of the picture with the rest of the men, but now they were out numbered to the point that any kind of confrontation would be extremely dangerous for him and Lisa.

They decided to follow the five men anyway, hoping for some kind of chance to come up that would give them an edge. Things quickly turned against them. As careful as Mack was following the SUV, the driver of it spotted Mack behind him. He couldn't be sure who it was behind him, but he was sure he didn't like the fact that someone was following him. In order to check out what was going on, the driver pulled over.

Mack didn't have much choice at that point and continued driving. As he went by the five men, the driver didn't like what he saw. With squealing tires, he pulled out from his parking spot and quickly closed the gap between himself and Mack.

They were soon on an empty piece of highway, with high rolling hills. Mack was the better of the two drivers, and knew how to handle those roads better than the other driver. While riding rodeo years before, Mack had a lot of practice driving the same kind of roads.

But he knew he would have to do something radical to win this battle. It was inevitable that as soon as the SUV was in position, the shooting would start. So Mack floored the accelerator. He managed to get far enough ahead to make his move. Using all his skill, he managed to spin himself around so he was facing the SUV.

He again floored the accelerator and aimed his vehicle at the SUV. The driver of it, suddenly realizing that Mack wasn't kidding, knew he had to try to dodge around Mack. He almost made it. Just as the two vehicles past each other, the rear quarter panel of Mack's vehicle clipped the SUV. The driver lost control and the car went into a hard spin, then flipped end over end. It managed three flips before it reached the steep cliff on the far side of the road. I bounced off the rocks of the cliff side before it finally exploded, and was fully engulfed in flames when it hit the bottom of the canyon it landed in.

"That certainly wasn't how I planned it, Lisa," Mack said. "But I guess it'll have to do."

"It's too bad when anyone has to die," she said. "But better them than us. So what's next? Check things in Tucson, or hope this is over and head back home?"

"Tucson. We've come this far, so let's make sure we've taken care of it before we go back home. Besides, I kind of like this part of the world, so we can make it a visit of sorts while we're here too."

"I'd like that, Mack. I kind of like it here too. And when all is said and done, we could both use a little rest."

Chapter 24

R oy and Wanda made their destination in Canada early in the afternoon of their second day out. They found and registered at a motel. After settling in their room, they went out to eat. They knew it was too late in the day to go looking for the man who found Jeffry Carro's body in his pasture.

Even with an address and directions that Sue had found for them after she did some thorough internet research, along with using GPS, they still knew it would be a good idea to have plenty of daylight to look for the man. They were sure too, that Larry Jameson was pretty much of a recluse, and was far more likely to be home when they got there than anywhere else.

That left them with several hours to fill before it would be time to go to bed for the night. To use up the time, they first wandered around the town, looking in store windows and making note of all of the eating establishments, no matter what type they were.

They'd covered most of the small town when, as they were crossing a street, a police car pulled up in front of them and stopped. A cop got out. "I'm curious," he said, "as to what you folks are doing in our town?"

"Killing time," Roy answered.

"What the hell do you mean? That was no answer. When I ask a question of a person, I expect an answer."

"And you got one," Roy answered. "You asked what we are doing and I told you."

"Killing time? That ain't no answer. Not the way you two been snooping around, looking everything over. So what the hell are you up to?"

"Absolutely not a damn thing. We just got here. Tomorrow we plan to do some exploring and maybe some hiking out in all the wild places around here. If we like it, we might stay a couple of days. If not, we'll be moving on. Either way, we've got some time to kill this afternoon, so we're taking a walk to use up that time. Beats the hell out of sitting in a motel room."

"That don't sound right to me," the cop complained. "If you like the wilderness the way you claim, why ain't you out camping, the way most folks would be?"

"We like to visit the wilderness, not live in it. Food's generally better in a restaurant too. Not to mention, we both like a big, soft bed."

"You're one of them what's always got an answer, ain't you!" The cop was getting frustrated. Roy wasn't full of fear the way he wanted him.

"You said you wanted answers to your questions. I gave you answers."

"You're a smart ass too. From the states, I can tell. All you people think you're such hot shit."

"Now that you've interrogated us and insulted us, are you done? We'd like to grab something to eat now. That is, if it's legal for a couple from Minnesota to eat in a restaurant in this town?"

"Go ahead, for now." The cop paused long enough to give them the evil eye. "But you'd best mind your manners," he added, "because I'll be watching you." With that final threat, he got in his car and drove away.

"I damn sure hope they aren't all that bad," Roy said as he left.

"Me too," Wanda agreed, "but don't get your hopes up. You know how it can be in some of these small towns."

"I do, and I know that there's not a damn thing we can do about it, beyond putting up with it. What do you say about going back to the motel, taking a shower and putting on some fresh clothes. I think we'll feel better after that long ride today if we do that."

"That sounds like a real good idea, Roy."

Wanda always liked to look good for Roy when they went out, no matter how simple the occasion. So after her shower she combed her hair and put it into a ponytail. She slipped on a pair of Levis just tight enough to make it obvious that she had a good figure, but not tight enough to show off too much. For her top, she put on a nice, short sleeve blouse, but also opted for comfort and left the bra in her suitcase.

When they left the motel, she was a very attractive women, just sexy enough to be noticed, but not as likely to be approached by any aggressive men. At least, not most places. This town, however, was loaded with young, single men, who worked at several different jobs out in the woods. Jobs that required a lot of hard, physical work.

They were also men who tended to be more than normal macho male crude, and very much tended to lack any female companionship. As soon as Wanda and Roy sat down at their table and the waitress gave them their menus, two of those crude men sat down with them. Roy instantly knew they were going to be trouble. Wanda did too, and she decided right then that she was going to put up with nothing from either one of the jerks.

"You people from out of town?" the biggest of the jerks asked.

"We don't want any trouble," Roy told him, "but we don't want any company either. So I suggest you move on."

"Hey, we're just trying to be friendly."

"No, you are not. You sat down because you are foolish enough to think you can make some kind of move on my wife. Forced or otherwise. It ain't gonna happen. Now get your asses the hell away from us and let us eat in peace. Before I'm forced to move you."

"You're awful mouthy for someone whose alone," the smaller to the jerks said. "You ain't careful, and you could damn well get yourself hurt."

"Maybe we could," Wanda snarled at them. "But it won't be from either one of you punks. Now get the hell away from our table before we are forced to hurt you." She glared at the smaller one. "And if I do some hurting, it's going to be you. I don't plan on stopping with any small hurt either. When I finish, you will know that it's always best to mind your manners."

"I think it's time," the smaller one said to the bigger one, "to teach these folks some manners."

Roy and Wanda stood up. Wanda was the one to answer them. "Bring it on. Now's a good a time as any."

Now the two big, macho males saw the look on Roy's face. It told them they might be pushing it too far. Then they met Wanda's eyes, and they knew without any doubt at all that the only smart thing to do was to make a hasty retreat. So they did.

"I'm almost disappointed," Wanda said. "I'm so sick and tired of guys like them, that I was looking forward to beating the hell out of one of them."

"I know what you mean, Wanda," Roy answered. "I feel the same way. We've always had too much of that kind of shit, but since Trump it's gotten a lot worse. If the president can do it, then every man should be able to. Even in Canada where he ain't president."

"Well, it's probably best they left. Given how that cop reacted to us earlier, if there was a fight, it's likely they'd blame us for it."

"Odds are, Wanda, that's exactly what they'll do before the night's over."

"Why? There was no fight."

"I hate to tell you this, Wanda, but it's my guess that what those two chickenshit assholes are doing right now is getting together with friends of theirs. There'll be a bunch of them waiting for us when we leave here."

"Maybe it would be a good idea to leave before they get back then."

"It might. But then, we'll have to be looking behind us the whole time we're here. Even if we do, odds are sooner or later they'll catch up with us. As much as I hate the idea, I think we might as well settle this tonight. But not until after we eat. They can stand out there and wait a while for us."

"You think then, Roy, they'll have help and will start a fight out there then?"

"Unless we can talk our way out of it, yes." Roy's face dropped into a tight grimace. "The thing is, if there is a fight, don't stay with one guy. Whoever you're facing, hurt him or take him out as quickly as you can. Then move on to the next once. They've got every chance of beating us, but we want them to pay dearly for it. And if they win. we'll settle it with them later, one macho jerk at a time."

"Do you think they'll rape me?"

"I hope not. But I will kill each and everyone of them if they do."

"Not if I get to them first.'

The waitress came then and took the orders for their meals. As they ate their food, they tried to look out the front windows. It was too dark to see anything, but there were two things going on. Six men had gathered in front of the restaurant. They were passing around a bottle of cheap Canadien whiskey as they laughed and bragged about what they planned on doing to the mouthy woman they were waiting for.

On the other side of the street, while loading up his pickup from the general store, Larry Jameson was watching the activity in front of the restaurant. He was there so late because he wanted, as much as possible, to avoid people.

Since the owner of the store knew Larry from the time he was a child, and had total respect for him and the way he lived, he did his best to accommodate Larry and the late hours he shopped. Larry and the general store owner were just finishing when Roy and Wanda left the restaurant.

The six men quickly surrounded Roy and Wanda. Larry knew trouble was in the making, and he had no doubt that the cause of the trouble was the six men. As much as he hated the idea of getting involved, he couldn't let things just happen. He hurried across the street and moved inside the circle of men.

Even though he was in his seventies, the general store owner knew he had to back Larry. His own good conscious wouldn't allow him to do otherwise. He grabbed an axe handle from a barrel of them just inside the store and joined Larry in the circle.

Larry spoke up then. "I don't know what you punks thought you were going to do to these folks, but your plans have been changed. It will be a good idea for you to move the hell on out of here now."

The bigger of the two men who started the trouble, answered, "This ain't no business of yours, so you can just butt out. It's all between us and these two mouthy assholes who don't even live around here."

"Six against two. I don't think so."

"If we have to," the trouble maker said, "we can just as well take all four of you out. Ain't no one but you can fight anyway. Except maybe this other guy, but I doubt it. It's a damn sure thing that this old man with a stick can't fight, and that woman is just going to be fun to wrestle with. At least, for a start. Later on it'll be more than just wrestling."

That remark was more than Wanda was willing to listen to without responding. She moved up on the man and pushed him. He staggered back and she did it again. After the third time, she lifted her hands in front of her and waved her fingers, inviting him to attack her. It was the same move she'd made on the guys in the bar at Track And Trail.

The guy stood there, his mouth hanging open, temporarily at a loss for words. "Come and get me," Wanda hissed at him. "I'm here. Come on and do to me what you planned on doing."

He finally decided to respond. He was furious over the way she talked to him. Everyone there could sense the contempt in her voice. As he moved in with his anger in total control of him, he left himself open for nearly anything she might decide to do to him.

She, however, was now in full control of not only herself, but the situation. She knew that there were a lot of fancy moves she could make to leave him looking beyond just stupid. Instead, she wisely decided to simply take him out. Hard enough so he stayed out. She kicked him in the groin with everything she had in her. The blow landed so hard, everyone there imagined that they heard a crunch when it did.

When he doubled over, her knee came up hard as she pulled the back of his head down. This time there was a crunch. It came from his nose being very broken. She looked each of the five men left in the eye, a grim smile on her face. She lifted her hands again and waved her fingers. "Which one of you totally chickenshit, useless little boys wants to do it to me next?" She gave them a full face evil grin. "I'm sure you are all at least as tough as your big bad friend here on the ground, so damn it, come and get me."

None of them had the slightest idea any longer, how to respond to her. Like their friend, they too had their mouths hanging open. Tired of the whole scene, Roy decided to react. He moved close to the second of the original troublemakers and snapped him under the chin with the side of his hand.

"Be a good idea to close your mouth," he said, "before it gets full of flies." He pushed the man. "Time to take your buddies and get the hell and gone out of here."

One of the four men who had been quiet the whole time, finally spoke. "No," he said, "we ain't going no wheres. You are. You and that bitch you call a wife. We live here. This is our town. We belong here. You don't. So it's you who will be moving on tonight. Back to wherever it is you come from."

Larry put in his opinion of the whole episode then. "But I do live here," he growled, "and these folks are as of now, my guests. You want to be taking me on too?"

"We're going to just beat the hell out of you, is what we're going to do. And I mean every damn one of you. Especially the bitch. And when we finish with that, we'll start with the rest. When we get done with her, she'll damn well know what a real man's cock feels like."

It was the man from the general store who started the melee. He was the kind of man who hadn't been involved in any type of violent situation for nearly fifty years. But he found the talk of raping a woman to be about an abhorrent thing as he could think of. So he simply used his ax handle to tap the latest loudmouth on the top of the head. It wasn't hard enough to do any serious or permanent damage, but it was hard enough to render the man unconscious for a while.

With the odds now even, people wise, the four macho men were beginning to question the wisdom of pushing things any further. After all, the woman proved that without a doubt, she could handle herself. And the old man, who they all had initially considered worthless, was actually more than capable with the ax handle in his hand. Even though he consistently avoided people, Larry was well known enough for everyone of the men still standing to be afraid of him.

Roy was the unknown, but from the complete lack of fear in his face, it was enough to convince the men that even if the odds were equal, they were still out numbered. If there was a fight, they would lose it. So they started to walk away.

"Not so fast," Wanda told them. they stopped and she moved close to the troublemaker who was one of the two who started everything. She grabbed him by the arm and swung him around to face her. "I told you that if you started anything, I'd kick your sorry ass. So I think I'll do that now."

"I think, Ma'am," Larry said, "it'll be best to just let him go."

"I don't know. He said he had all sorts of plans for the things he was going to do to me. I think it'll be fun to fix him so he can't ever do any of that to any woman ever again."

"I can't help but agree with you, but still, it will be best for now, to just let him go. There's been enough trouble for one night."

Wanda shook her head, but didn't move.

Roy put an arm around her. "Maybe next time. But for now, let's call it a night."

She relented and they let the men leave. At Roy's suggestion, they went back into the restaurant to have a drink and get acquainted. The old man declined to join them, saying he needed to finish closing up his store and get home before is wife worried. Larry was reluctant. It was a long time since he'd been in a bar in this town. But he went in with them anyway.

Once they were settled at the bar inside, Roy and Wanda ordered beers and Larry ordered soda water. As they talked they soon discovered that they all had a lot of interests in common.

They didn't stay at the bar long, but before they left it, Larry convinced Roy and Wanda that it would be safest for them to stay with him, at least for the coming night. Roy agreed, if for no other reason than he'd figured out who Larry was. The man, and the main reason they were in Canada.

Sometime in the morning, he would tell Larry who they were, and try to talk to him about finding the body of Jeffry Carro. He just hoped Larry wouldn't get too upset when he learned who they were.

Chapter 25

Carson Chambers was elated. The message he'd just received, from his recently hired operatives in Canada, was filled with good news. Two of the people he was after, were apparently there. They were snooping around, and had only narrowly avoided getting beaten up in a bar fight with some of the local boys.

What made him so joyful about what he learned was knowing where the woman was. She was one of the two. Capturing her, and having her brought to a place he owned, which had complete privacy, was what he wanted most.

He needed her desperately now. The thought of taking and using a woman like that did things for him even his daughter, at her best, didn't do. That woman, after all, could shoot better than all but a very few men on the entire planet. She could fight. And from what had been described to him, she proved that she fought better than most men.

He was sure, in his own mind, that once he had her under his control, she would know her best chances. Which would be to give him, the superior man, what he had coming. And given the powerful woman she was, he was certain that she would give him a ride like few men had ever known.

But now, sitting at his desk in total anticipation for the things the miracle woman was going to do for him, he couldn't wait. He thought of having one of the many willing women (they were all paid well for their extra service) brought in to service him, but decided against it. No matter which one it was, she would disappoint him.

He took himself in hand, he concentrated on the image he'd created in his mind of the mystery woman. He quickly brought himself to the place that he could never satisfy until he actually had her. But he continued to try several times that day. Sometimes by hand, and sometimes with a woman. It did little good for him. He still went home frustrated that night.

He thought about his daughter in the hospital, and considered visiting her, but decided against it. He knew that trying to use her there to ease his needs would not be acceptable there. Add to that, right now she was really ugly with all the bandages on her face.

Thinking about her only made his situation worse. All he could do about his daughter was hope when she healed, she didn't have too many scars. It would be a pure tragedy for him if she ended up looking too ugly for him to use in the future.

But then again, if he offered enough money, he should be able to convince the super woman into staying with him permanently. If staying with him, giving him what he wanted and needed, could make her rich. Very very rich, actually, why wouldn't she want to. Add to that, he was handsome and really good in bed, so he was certain she would.

But those thoughts made him edgy again. He quickly contacted the man in Canada, and one more time reaffirmed what he wanted. The women was to be personally delivered, totally unharmed and not in any way violated. When it happened, the people there in Canada would have three million dollars to share.

It was a small fortune for them, he knew, but for him, it was little more than small change. This was something else about life that constantly surprised him The difficulty most people had with money. Everyone should be able to do what he did. Invest their inheritance wisely and gather in the money. Sure, you needed to keep track of it, but that's all. It had all been so easy for him, and that made it true for him that it would be easy for everyone.

Thinking about his money, made him think about how he spent it. That made him think about his wife. He allowed her a large allowance, but it had been a long time since she'd given anything in return. Since nothing right now could give him the kind of satisfaction he wanted, he decided he would try her out again. Who knew, maybe she could be at least a little like her daughter. If she was, it might give him some minimal satisfaction.

He found her in bed. She was with the youngest of their three gardeners. "What the hell," he said when he entered her room.

"No," she said, a bit of a smile on her face. "Not hell at all. Pretty good actually. Why don't you be nice, Carson, and wait in the hall for a little bit. Then we can talk."

Feeling quite strange about it, he did. It was a short wait. As soon as the gardener left the room, he joined his wife. He expected to be angry when he saw her. Instead, he found himself wanting her. They didn't talk at all when he joined her in bed.

After, he felt like some of the pressure he was feeling all day was lifted. He let her watch when he called Canada again. "Just to be sure," he said, "I'm going to raise your fee to bring me the woman safely to four million. Make damn sure I get her the way I want her."

The man in Canada was now excited beyond what he believed possible. Four million went way past anything he'd ever even dreamed of. Add to that, he was the only one who knew the true numbers. If he kept the split with the others to two million, they'd all still be happy. And after all was said and done, he could leave this small town with his extra two million, and move to a big city.

But first, he had to come up with a plan that offered a way to kill the husband, yet keep the wife totally unharmed. It was something he knew would be difficult, but not at all impossible. As much as he wanted to do the bitch before he turned her in, he could forget her for that much money.

Chapter 26

Lisa and Mack were now enjoying their time in Tucson. They'd checked around some, and had even attended one of Joseph's churche's daily services. It didn't seem as though much of anything special was going. Not anything dealing with them anyway.

The young man who held the service didn't seem concerned at all about Joseph's absence. It was far more that he simply enjoyed being in charge, and Joseph, wherever he was, was an unnecessary component of the church. Something he was happy enough to be rid of.

Mack and Lisa found reassurance in the fact that they completely escaped any kind of notice during or after the service. They then decided to turn the visit to a vacation of sorts, and explored the sites in the Tucson area. That put them where they were now. On the old Mount Lemon road that ran through the Catalina mountains, from the town of Oracle to Summer Haven. It was a mostly two lane, dirt road on the top of the mountain. It was only considered safe for a four wheel drive vehicle.

That was no problem for Mack. They were back in his pickup, and it was four wheel drive. The back was filled with enough equipment to somewhat even out the weight, so it was relatively easy going for them.

It proved to be a beautiful drive, and so different from the the layout of the mountain on the Tucson side. It was the kind of thing that if a person didn't know any better, it could be taken for a different mountain range.

Much of it was grassland, loaded with cattle. It was open range, and with Lisa's insistence, they frequently stopped so she could pet some animal or the other. Along with the cattle, there were horses, mules, donkeys, and ponies. Lisa liked them every bit as much as the cattle.

The deer, up so high on those mountains, were a lot more shy than the ones they encountered in the Rincon Mountains on their first trip to Arizona. So they only saw them off in the distance.

Another critter they saw, only at a distance, was a large, probably male, brown bear. He, like the deer, wanted nothing to do with them. They did see a few lizards that they couldn't identify, but that was about it for wildlife. They were somewhat disappointed because of that, but at the same time did very much appreciate the scenery along the entire drive.

Since they took their time, the drive used up a good part of the day. They then decided to find a good Mexican restaurant and enjoy a good meal before giving it up for the day.

They found one off the normal beaten path that looked interesting. It proved to be just that. The best thing of all were their burritos. They gave the customer the option of building their own. Because they were fascinated by the concept, they both ordered them with so many ingredients they couldn't finish them. Not even with the large appetites they both had. Luckily, their motel room came with a small refrigerator, so they could hold the leftovers until the next day.

In the morning they decided to just get in the truck and randomly drive around. They knew that somewhere they would find a cafe for breakfast. And Tucson being the kind of city it was, they wouldn't have any trouble finding something to do to fill in the day.

They didn't get far though, before Mack's mirror was filled with blue lights and a short blip of a siren going off. He immediately pulled over. His stomach did a little flip as he thought about the car full of five men rolling down a cliff. He knew though, the odds of anyone connecting that incident to him or Lisa was extremely slight.

He didn't have to wonder long about why he was pulled over. The cop who made the stop walked up to Mack with full confidence. He wore a smile when Mack rolled down the window.

He introduced himself, then said, "I remember you from a while back. You two were the ones who ended up in a gunfight with a guy we screwed up and let loose when we shouldn't have. I was kind of surprised to see you back here in Tucson so soon. I decided then, to be nosey and ask you why. I hope I didn't make you too nervous."

"No problem," Mack told him. "I used to occasionally do the same thing back when I was still a cop."

Mack's comment that said he was no longer a cop, surprised the cop he was talking to. He took a step back. "Are you saying you quit being a cop? Why the hell would you do that?"

Mack went ahead and told him the whole story about the problems with the commissioners. He finished with, "and since we've both got some time off, we decided to take a vacation. We kind of fell in love with this part of the country while we were here, so this where we decided to go."

"That's something, quitting your jobs in protest It took a lot of guts. You might not get them back now though."

"Probably not. Thing is, we were getting tired of being shot at anyway. And in the long run, we'll find something to do."

"You two seem like good people, so I'm sure you will. Right now though, I was going to ask you if you knew anything about three missing people. Two of them are from your part of the world, and the third one originally was. The thing is, the one who lived here is a preacher of sorts. He's also the father of the man you shot, ma'am."

"Don't look at me," Lisa answered, vigorously shaking her head. "I don't plan on shooting or otherwise killing anyone. In fact, the killing part is what made it easier to quit my job than what it otherwise would have been."

"Don't worry yourself none. I didn't think for one minute you had anything to do with him going missing. I just pulled you over to see what you are doing here. I brought up about them missing only so I could ask you to keep your eyes open while you're moving around. Seems like there's too many people going missing who never did show up here. There's a couple of guys from out east too. Seems as though some one of those multi-billionaires is screaming fire 'cause they're missing."

"That shouldn't be any surprise to you," Mack answered. "You know how people with money are. They think they own all of us. We aren't anything more that something to kick around."

"So true, but as nice as it is to talk with you guys, I'd best get rolling. The boss likes us to keep moving."

"That was a surprise," Lisa said as Mack pulled back on the road. He did us a favor though. Now we know that no one's found those five yet."

"That doesn't surprise me. No one can see the wreck from the highway. It's a deep canyon where their car landed, so it might not be found until a hiker or someone like that accidentally runs across it. The thing is though, the law knows we are here now, so I think we'll only give it a couple more days. By then it'll be time to head back home."

"You're right, Mack. The longer we're gone when they do find that car with those five bodies in it, the less likely anyone will think about us in connection with it."

"Yeah, even though what we did was only self defense, the less legal stuff we have to go through, the better. Now, let's hunt up something to do."

They finally decided on something fun, but very easy to do. They decided to drive the wildlife drives in both sections of Saguaro National Park. They started on the west side.

The ride there was a pleasant one, and once they were free of Tucson itself, they drove through some rugged terrain. They could see how beautiful it must have been at one time. Now, it was still a scenic drive, but it left a lot to be desired. Too much of the landscape was filled with homes that could only be owned by millionaires, or those even richer.

To most people, the homes were a thing of beauty, and the people living in them were to be envied. To Mack and Lisa, they were a form of pollution that was permanent. As much as any public dump, they represented a lot of what the human race was doing on its hell bent race to destroy the earth itself.

As much as the display of all that money disturbed them, they were bound and determined to find some joy in their day. They managed to shake off a lot of the distaste, created in their mouths from the mini-mansions crowding out the beautiful, natural landscape, to enjoy the wildlife drive. They especially enjoyed the saguaro cactus. Something nearly every visitor to any of that part of the world did.

Tucson and its surrounding area was all part of the Sonora Desert. The landscape was unique to itself, and quite unlike any other desert. Often, when the fall and winter rains are sufficient, the desert goes into full bloom in the spring. It can last for months as the plants in bloom change from one species to another.

There were no flowers now, but rain had been heavy enough for the land to offer a lot of green, and it was beautiful in its own right. Enough that they could set aside the letdown feeling given to them from driving through the large area of mini-mansions.

When they left the west side and drove to the wildlife drive in the eastern portion of Saguaro National Park, they again found a lot of homes pushing close to the park. They were for the most part large, and priced out of the reach of the average person. But at least one could be less than a millionaire to own one.

The drive itself was a bit more hilly than the one on the west side, and was in its own way even more beautiful. They stopped in a small parking area provided and walked to a trail filled with giant saguaro cactus. Several of them were huge, and probably over a hundred and fifty years old.

They both marveled at the size, and were grateful to the people who managed to save them. They wondered though, how much longer they would be part of the landscape. This was the world of Trump. He and the rest of the Republicans were hell bent on destroying as much of what little preserved land there was, as they possibly could.

Thinking about it, Mack had no doubt that they would eventually manage to sell off most places like this. In a world of Trump and Republicans, there was simply no tolerance for anything that benefited the average citizen. If it wasn't for the rich, it was worthless.

Chapter 27

C arson Chambers was no longer in a good mood. His Canada people still hadn't made any move on his mystery woman and her husband. It was frustrating him. He wasn't at all used to being kept waiting when he wanted something, and this was something he really wanted.

It was seldom in his life, that he couldn't get what he wanted when he wanted it. All it took was money. But it didn't seem to be doing the job this time. What could be so damn complicated about grabbing one woman and delivering her to him.

The part about killing the husband was even simpler. He knew, he'd had it done a few times in the past. But then, those people from Canada were a different breed. It could be that they just didn't have the proper respect for a man of his stature. He would have to watch them closely on this matter. If, in the end, he wasn't satisfied with their performance, he could and would use a small part of his billions to destroy their already useless little town.

And if they failed to deliver his mystery woman to him in the condition he demanded, all of his current operatives working on that problem directly would surely have to die. For him to not receive delivery of her, and in a timely manner, would be for him a personal disaster. He rarely actually needed anything, but for some driving reason, he desperately needed her. His imagination was now too stimulated for him to accept anything less.

Then, the thought of a disaster brought to mind the two men who were sent out to eliminate Mack and Lisa Thomas, who were now missing. They just disappeared. One minute they were on the trail of those two constant trouble makers. The next minute they seemed have disappeared from the face of the earth.

What could have happened to them. They were professionals who had completed dozens of jobs just like that one. Most of those jobs had been even more difficult than taking out two people who were essentially nothing but a couple of country bumpkins.

So what the hell happened to his men? He couldn't see how, in any way, those two annoying, simple minded people, could have had a damn thing to do with their disappearance.

His large personal staff were watching news reports from everywhere the men could have been, and there was no kind of disaster or murder that could have been about them.

The only thing that caught anyone's attention at all, was the disappearance of three other men. One of them a preacher, who coincidentally, was the father of a man Lisa had shot and killed a few months prior to this activity.

The car the three men were driving was also found outside a motel where they stayed one night. All four tires of the car were slashed. But there was no direct evidence to show that Mack and Lisa had been there. Only that a couple no one could describe had stayed the night.

As difficult as it was to admit, even to himself, he was beginning to wonder if there wasn't something more to Mack and Lisa than he previously thought. It didn't take much soul searching on his part, to contact the people he kept on retainer. After a short conversation, he had their guaranty that if they couldn't bring him Mack and Lisa alive so he could deal with them his way, they would supply him with authentic photos of their dead bodies.

Since Carson was now in such a serious need of his mystery woman, he agreed to the terms, imperfect as they were. He then paced the floor of his office, pondering the two problems he was facing. It seemed to be an awful lot of trouble, caused by only two couples.

Where did the mystery woman and her errant husband come from. It seemed as though she especially, came from nowhere. With all the chaos those four had managed to cause, it almost seemed as though they should be related. But that was something he knew was impossible. No one family could possibly cause so much trouble.

As he paced, constantly fretting over his now personal problems, his need for something to ease the pressure building inside him was constantly growing.

He wanted to use his daughter in the worst way, and if she were home from the hospital, he would do that. He considered using one of the over paid women in his office, but they were better suited for different times. His wife might help some, but she was always so busy with her three gardeners, that she just didn't any longer provide the emotional support she once was so good at it.

It was a last resort, but one he was sure would provide some easing of his constant tension. Since he couldn't have her, he needed someone as much like his daughter as he could find.

He called a contact he knew. They in turn made the arrangements. He took the elevator to the basement garage. There, he got into the back seat of a waiting car. After a ten minute drive he was dropped off in another basement garage.

"I'll come back when they call," the driver said, then drove away.

He took the elevator again, and got off on the tenth floor. He exited the elevator into a moderately sized waiting room. After a moments wait, a young woman, dressed almost modestly, took his elbow.

"I'll take you to her," she said in a soft, soothing voice. "We are sure you will like her."

The girl in the room he entered was laying down in the center of a king size bed. Her only dress was a skimpy, see through night gown. She was pretty, and even though her smile was very much forced, he liked her. She so much reminded him of his daughter Shanty. Fifteen years ago, she had looked very much like this girl.

It was her age that did it, Carson was sure. Close to the age Shanty was when he started with her. Twelve, maybe thirteen years old.

Chapter 28

When Roy got up for his always middle of the night pee call, he decided to go out on Larry's deck to take in some night air. He was also feeling restless, and didn't want to disturb Wanda by going back to bed too quickly. It surprised him to find Larry already there, leaning on the railing and starring out into the woods surrounding the property.

"If my coming out here this time of the night bothers you," Roy told him, "I can go back to bed."

Larry chuckled. "No problem. I suspect you're up for the same reason I am. Seems like us men don't have to get very old, before our bladder doesn't function quite as good as we'd like."

Roy shook his head. "I don't know about most men, but it's been a pain for a long time. One that I'm used to now though."

"Ah well, since it got both of us up, it might be a good time to talk some. We haven't done much of that since we met."

"That's a good idea," Roy said. "We've been planning to talk to you in the morning. As you probably already figured out, we aren't here to go hiking. We are here to see you. It was a pleasant surprise when we discovered last night that you are who you are."

"Why would you come all the way here from Minnesota just to see me? I'm nobody important. I just try to keep to myself and stay the hell out of everyone's way. I don't like trouble. I saw enough of too many kinds of trouble in my life already."

"I can understand and appreciate that. We're here about the body you found in your pasture." Roy went on to tell him about what he and Wanda were doing now. He also explained the work for the sister of

Jeffry Caro, and how she wanted to learn about his death. From there, he explained about the ethics and standards his family intended to make part of their detective agency.

"You mean," Larry said, his tone of voice carrying a tone of a hint of disbelief, "you plan to solve the case for that sister, even if you lose money at it? You don't plan on staying in business very long, do you?"

"Actually, we do. For a lot of reasons I'd prefer to explain at some other time, none of us involved in the company needs to make a whole lot of money. Part of that is because we don't want that much."

"That sounds pure and noble and all," Larry said, "but none of it explains what it is that you want out of me."

"The thing is, Larry, there isn't anything specific that we want. Mostly, what we are hoping for is the chance to talk to you. You're doing that now, so this conversation is the start of what we want from you."

"I have to admit, that's simple enough. But I'm finally getting a bit tired now. I think I'll crawl back in, and get some sleep. You don't mind if we pick this up in the morning, do you?"

"Not at all. The morning's as good a time as any."

Roy was tired now too, but even so, Wanda felt really soft and warm when he settled in the bed. He held her close on his way to finding some sleep.

It didn't last long. Less than an hour after he fell asleep, Roy and Wanda were suddenly awakened by several male voices screaming obscenities. The locals from town were outside wanting to exact their revenge, he was sure, for the previous nights activities.

He and Wanda quickly dressed, which included strapping their hand guns to their waist. They met Larry in the small living room of his house.

Before they could talk, one of the men outside yelled, "Send out the woman. We guaranty she won't be harmed. Then we can settle this without her being part of it. We don't want her hurt."

Roy looked at Larry, then at the rifle in his hand. "You have any more of those?" he asked.

"Just one. I'll get it for you."

"Give it to Wanda. She can outshoot the both of us."

"You sure about that?" Larry looked skeptical. "Damn few men can outshoot me."

"The one thing I know. She doesn't miss. She is better than me, so give her the gun."

"Before I do, I think we should consider the fact that she might be better off out there. She'll be out of the line of fire that way."

"Maybe. But she'll be better off dead than living through what will ultimately happen to her. Unless she says otherwise, she stays."

"Fine by me," he said. He got the rifle for Wanda, then stepped out the front door. He looked over the group of men out there. There were seven of them. "I know every goddamn one of you," he told them, his tone of voice dripping with contempt. "So when this is over, I will swear out a warrant for the arrest of every one of you still alive. If you want to stay alive and out of jail, you'll be on your way home shortly."

"You know we can't do that," the man who asked for Wanda to come out said. He raised his rifle and fired at Larry. He was as good with his rifle as he was at everything in his life. He missed him completely.

Larry moved back inside. As he did, a second shot rang out. One of the outside men screamed, and that was followed by six more shots and additional screams. The seven men, who were bunched together out in the open while Larry was out there, were now bunched together on the ground. They each now carried a nonfatal bullet somewhere in their body.

Before they could do anything more to the men, Wanda came downstairs. "None of them are dead," she said, "so be careful when you go out there to check on them. They might still be armed. You might tell them, since it's true that none of them are too bright, that if I'm forced to shoot them again, next time I do, I will kill them."

"Jesus Christ, Woman," Larry nearly shouted, "you already shot all seven of them with just seven shots?"

"I was being careful, so I shot each one of them individually. Most times, a situation like that, I should have taken them out with about four shots. I figured though, it's better to use a few more bullets than taking any chances on missing one of them."

Larry looked at Roy, shaking his head. "You were right. She damn sure can outshoot me."

"I think she even outdid herself this time," Roy said, a grin on his face. "I suppose though, we ought to go out there and check on those fools. We wouldn't want any of them to bleed to death. At least not before the law gets a look at them."

None of the men bled enough to kill them. It was obvious who was attacking who, so Wanda was off the hook as far as criminal charges were concerned. None of the cops could accept the fact that she was the shooter anyway.

All but one of the seven men refuse to talk or answer even the simplest questions. The one who talked complained that Larry, Roy, and Wanda weren't the only people in the house. The shooting came so fast that there had to have been at least a dozen men shooting.

Then he complained some more. "That damn billionaire, Carson Chambers, sending us out here to get all shot up, just 'cause he's got the hots for some mystery broad. According to him, she's worth millions, just to spend time in his bed. Says doing her will be the greatest sex ever. Just 'cause she can shoot and fight, she's gonna serve him better in bed that any other woman ever could."

Roy knelt on the ground close to the man. "Are you saying then, that Carson Chambers hired you to come out here and kidnap my wife?"

"That was part of it, yes. Killing you and Larry, that was the other part. He's pissed 'cause of all the trouble you and your wife caused him. You and some of them other folks from Minnesota. But pissed or not, he sure does want to put his hands all over that wife of yours. And the hell of it all, is the damn fact he doesn't even know who the hell she is. Only stories about what she's done. But he damn sure is determined to have her. So you can expect there'll be more men after her. He ain't gonna quit until she belongs to him."

When Roy told Wanda what the man said, all she could do was shake her head in disbelief. "Of all the damn fool things I've ever heard, this has to be it. Some billionaire is willing to spend millions to kidnap me. And why? Only because I can shoot. If he ever does get his hands on me, Roy, you can believe me when I say, I will kill him. No matter what it takes."

Roy and Wanda decided to stay one more day, to have a chance to talk further with Larry. They had found now, that they really liked the man. He was straight forward and honest, and didn't expect much from life beyond his basic personal needs.

Along with those attributes, he had a deep love of nature and full respect for the environment. In short, he was very much like the Thomas family. Everything about him them, made him a very easy person to be around.

Their day passed by quickly, and they were close to bringing it to an end. But just before they moved to go inside the house and retire for the night, a car drove up. It was the chief cop from town. It was easy to see the concern written on his face as he walked up to them. He nodded to Roy and Wanda, then turned to Larry.

"I hate having to tell you this," he said, "but there's trouble brewing in town. Way too many folks are upset about what went down last night. I know just as well as you do, that those men were the problem, not you. That doesn't change the feelings floating among them though. I'm here to warn you. I'd tell you to be prepared, except there's too much unrest now. I think it would be best if you just leave. You can probably return in a month or so, Larry." He turned to Roy. "Unfortunately, for you, a permanent stay away from here would be the best thing for you to do."

Roy shook his head in disgust. "People can sure get the wrong idea in their heads from not knowing what things are really about. This started when I refused to let a couple of drunken perverts mess with my wife. Then we get that billionaire lusting after her so bad he wants to have Larry and I killed just so he can get at her. And it's all our fault. What a bunch of total bullshit."

"I won't even begin to argue with you on that, but it'll still be a good idea for you to get the hell out of here. I plain don't have the manpower it will take to protect you. Not to mention a lot of my deputies agree with the idea that you caused the problems, no one else. So, if for no other reason than the protection of your wife, I think you should move on."

"As much as I hate letting someone do this to me," Roy decided, "this time I think you're right."

Wanda gave them her thoughts on the subject then. "I don't like this either, Roy," she explained. "But right now, I really don't feel like spending the rest of my life in a jail in a foreign country just because I killed half a town full of jackasses. So let's pull out tonight. It'll be best for Larry too."

"You're right, Wanda," Larry agreed. "It'll be best all around if we all pull out tonight."

"Where are you going to go, Larry?" Roy asked.

"Don't know for sure, but I'll probably camp out up in the hills somewhere. The weather will be decent for a while yet. Maybe by the time it's not, it'll be safe to dome back." He looked at the cop. "You'll find homes for all my critters, won't you?"

"I will, and I'll keep a close eye on your place while you're gone. I'll do my best to keep it safe."

"I appreciate that."

"You know what, Larry," Roy said, "instead of camping this time, I think you should come with us. We've got plenty of room, and you might find our way of living interesting. At least for a while."

"I don't know. I'm no longer used to being around lot of people." He sighed heavily. "No, that's not quite true. I'm not used to being around any people."

"That shouldn't matter. Until you get used to us, there's plenty enough room to get lost in. We'll give you all the time you need to adjust."

"I know this is going to sound crazy coming from me," Wanda said, "but there's a very pretty young lady there, who might like making a new friend. Now, keep in mind I said only said friend. But there are days and times when I think she could use one not so close as all of us are."

"There's some truth to that. As good a friend as she is to Wanda and me, there are those days."

"I'd give you an answer to all that," Larry said, "but I just don't have one now. Give me some time to think on it."

They agreed then, that Roy and Wanda would head on home, and that Larry would spend at least the next few days up in the hills, thinking about what to do next.

Chapter 29

Mack and Lisa decided to take one more hike before heading back to Minnesota. There was still one mountain range close to Tucson they'd never explored. The Santa Ritas. They drove southeast of Tucson on I19, about forty miles, until they reach a small retirement city called Green Valley. From there they left the freeway and drove another ten to fifteen miles to a place called Madera Canyon. It was a gradual, but steady climb from the freeway to the canyon, so they were at a higher elevation when they entered the canyon.

It didn't seem like much when they got out of Mack's pickup near the start of a trail called Old Baldy. But given how steep and rough the trail was, the thinner air did contribute to the difficulty of the steep climb up the trail.

As difficult as the climb was for them though, they both found it to be a beautiful hike. Up this high, the landscape was far different than that of the lower desert. Here, it was dominated by various species of needle bearing trees and various kinds of shrubs. There were few signs of desert plants.

All around were signs of large animals like deer and bear, even though they didn't see any. What they did see though, were a lot of species of insects and lizards that were new to them.

The trail also offered a constant stream of places with scenic views, some of which went on for miles. For Mack and Lisa, who were not at all acclimated to such vigorous exorcise at such a high elevation, those spots served as more than a place to enjoy the fantastic views. Every bit as important, they served as places for them to stop and catch their breath when the climb became too much.

They followed the trail as far as a place called Josephine Saddle. There they sat down and rested for a while. As they did, Mack's attention drifted from the scenic place they were, to Lisa. Her attention was focused on her surroundings, so she didn't notice that he was watching her closely.

As he did, he couldn't help but wonder at the fact that in the few years he'd known her, she'd grown from a pretty teenage girl, to a woman so unbelievably beautiful.

How, he wondered, could he be so lucky. To have her in his life was something that went beyond anything he'd ever expected from life just a short time ago.

When his thoughts carried him to the point he wished there were someplace real private close by he could take her, he knew it was time for them to resume their hike. He stood and took her hand.

"It's time to get moving," he said.

"Okay," she agreed as she let go of his hand and stretched. As she did, she looked at him, her eyes drifting up and down his body. She grinned. "What brought that on?" she asked, nodding in his direction.

He returned her grin with a sheepish one of his own. "The one thing that always does. You. Often when I look at you, I'm surprised. Then it happens. This time there's no one around, so we don't have to be embarrassed."

"I don't get embarrassed, Mack. It makes me proud. I've been in love with you since I learned what love is. I just hope that never stops happening to you."

He kissed her, again took her hand, and they started the hike down. Only this time they took the Super Trail. It was a longer hike than Old Baldy, but not near so steep. It was smoother, a bit wider, and all together an easier trail than Old Baldy.

They stopped often along the trail to enjoy the many scenic vistas, but still made it down in less time than the hike up took. When they got back to their motel, it was late in the day, so they decided to get some sleep right away. That way they could leave for home earlier than normal.

Lisa took a shower first. When Mack took his, he half expected she would be asleep by the time he got in the bed. She wasn't. "You don't need those clothes," she told him when he was ready to get into bed.

He shed what little he had on and got in the bed with her. She pulled him over her. "Ever since I saw what happened to you un in that mountain," she said, "I've been thinking about this. You don't have to wait. In fact, I don't want you to wait. I'm ready when you are."

He'd been thinking the same as she'd been. They joined together quickly, then followed with slow, soft sharing that only two who have already shared the way they did could do.

They kissed when their time came, then stayed linked together until sleep drifted over them. Only then did Mack slip off and to her side. She held him tight to her until they awakened hours later.

It was about four-thirty when they finished loading the truck and left the motel. Lisa curled up against the door the best she could with the seat belt on, and quickly fell asleep.

Mack didn't at all mind that she did. He'd had an excellent sleep. It seemed as though the comfort and love he got from her did more to enable him to sleep sound than anything else.

Because Lisa wasn't awake yet, he skipped the traditional stop at Texas Canyon and drove straight through to a truck stop they liked outside of Los Cruces. They needed gas by then, not to mention a rest room.

"Where are we?" Lisa wanted to know when he woke her up.

"Truck stop near Los Cruces."

"My god, I can't believe I slept that long."

"You must have been tired."

She chuckled. "Nah. I think I was just very well relaxed. Something happened to me last night that took away all my cares and woes. For a while anyway. I think I'll need a repeat tonight though."

"You'll have to earn it. You get to drive for a while."

"I'll be glad to, Mack."

The rest of the trip was routine. They stopped about halfway for the night. Lisa got her wish. Then they slept good and were on their way early again. They made it home by late afternoon.

Roy knew they were home right away, but gave them a couple of hours before he called them. "I know that you're probably tired," he told Mack when he answered, "but are you up for going out for a burger and fries?"

"Let me ask Lisa." He did and she was willing to go. They agreed on a time and met at the Mystic Curve Inn. As they almost always seemed to be, Mack and Lisa were the last ones there.

Mack had only expected to see Roy and Wanda, so he was surprised to see everyone who was part of their new detective agency. Not only that, there was someone there who had never come with him when he did anything dealing with police work. Detective Paul Danielson's wife was with him.

She spoke up when Mack and Lisa were seated. "I'm sure," she said, "that all of you are wondering what it is that I'm dong here now. I guess I could make my answer complicated, but I won't. I'm here because I want to tell you all that I fully support what you're trying to do. I realize that it's unlikely that I'll ever be of any direct help for your efforts, but again, I thought I should at least show my support."

"We appreciate that more than you know," Roy told her. "We need all the support we can get."

Everyone agreed to that, then Roy asked Mack and Lisa how their trip went.

"The problem with the church attacks on Lisa should be over," Mack explained. "And we managed to hand the billionaire a setback. Although I don't really expect that to last."

"And what is it that you did to manage all that?" Roy asked.

Mack shrugged his shoulders, sighed, then shook his head in frustration over the question. He knew it wouldn't be a good idea to answer it with any detail. It was something that was best forgotten, so the fewer people who knew the details the better.

He looked Roy in the eye and said, "There's no good way to say this, Roy, but I think it's best to leave it where it is. The church attacks on Lisa should be over. And now that I didn't properly answer your question, what can you tell me about your trip to Canada?"

"I understand, Mack" Roy said, his eyes showing Mack that he really did. "As far as going to Canada, it was a strange time to say the least." He went on to tell all of them about it, then finished with, "And can you believe it? An old man like me, married to a goddess. That billionaire is willing to spend many millions just to get his hands on her."

Wanda laughed, then said, "I'm anything but a goddess, even if you did treat me like one last nigh, Roy. And the way you did that, proves you're anything but an old man."

After the light laughter from Wanda's comment died, Paul joined the conversation. "From what I've been able to learn while you four were traveling, Chambers wants more than just getting his hands on Wanda. Although, she does seem to be his number one priority. It looks like he wants to get a hold of Mack and Lisa too. From what I could learn, he hopes to capture them alive, torture and rape Lisa while Mack is forced to watch, then kill them both."

"It's beginning to sound like we've got a serious problem with that Carson Chambers," Mack commented. "Anyone have any ideas on how we are going to deal with him."

"I've been trying to figure out a way," Paul said, "but I haven't come up with a decent idea yet. The problem, as I see it, is money. A billion dollars is more than any of us could spend on personal wishes in a lifetime. This guy has tens of billions of dollars. How the hell can we fight that? We all know that he can buy damn near anything."

"The truth is," Mack said, "we are all at least to some degree rich. But even if we pool all our recourses together, they amount to next to nothing compared to what that man has."

The ideas started to flow among them then, but a solution to their problem remained rather elusive, even though they talked late into the night. They didn't break up their meeting until they were told the place was closing.

They did, however, agree on one positive thing. It was time to tell their client, what they'd learned about her brother's death.

Her response was simple. "So he was killed by accident, and they covered it up anyway? Just so it didn't look bad for the guns or the company that made the one that killed him. What a bunch of total assholes those people are. I think I'll sue them. I might not win, but it might make the news, and if it does, they'll look twice as bad as they would have if they would have handled it properly in the first place. And if they had, maybe that idiot who shot him would still be alive. Then I could sue him too."

Mack could find no reason to disagree with her.

Chapter 30

The stories about the seemingly amazon woman who could now outshoot any man alive, and beat almost any five men in a fight, were running rampant around the Track And Trail club house.

Derrick James was reduced to nothing but nerves. Carson Chambers was making a habit of calling him every few hours, wanting to know if he'd learned anything new about his mystery woman. Of course, he hadn't learned a thing about her. Worse yet, he didn't know where to start looking. He'd even tried a couple of private detective agencies, but the two he hired got nowhere with the search. The third one turned him down.

He couldn't begin to understand why a new agency would turn him down that way. But there was a good reason. The agency was Refuge Rescuers, and they weren't about to take his money to find someone they didn't want found.

Then, in desperation, Derrick made an off the wall suggestion to Carson. "Maybe if you have some of your people go to Canada, they might find that guy up there who was with your mystery woman for a while."

"You know what, Derrick, you might have a good idea there. I hate spending so much money, but it might be the only way to do it."

"I shouldn't think the money would bother you. A couple hundred grand won't affect even one billion. Given what you have, it can't possibly have any effect on you."

"When it comes to money, Derrick, everything affects me. I didn't get where I am by throwing my money around without thinking about where each and every dollar goes."

"The thing is though, if they find him and he leads you to her, it will be money well spent. After all, she is your mystery dream woman, isn't she?"

"She is, so I think I'll take your advice on that. Your idea has given me one too. I need you to keep open three of your finest suites. I'll foot the bill for them. I'm going to be sending some of the best people that Life's Protection Corporation has on retainer. They can search for my mystery lady there too. Who knows, she might still be around there somewhere. Just as important though, I'm going to have them move on that Mack and Lisa Thomas couple. I still think we need to get them out of the picture. Not to mention, doing a full job on that Lisa would be a pure pleasure. As much as I hate her, I still think she is some babe."

"She is that, but from what I've heard about them, they are dangerous to screw with. A lot of people have tried in the past. So far, none of them have been successful."

"I think my track record of success speaks for itself. I didn't get where I am by making mistakes."

"No, you certainly didn't. But try to remember, hard as it might be, that money can't buy everything."

"Maybe not, but it's going to buy me everything I want out of this mess. All I have to do is spend enough of it, and I will get what I want."

"You're going to send some of your own people to Canada then?"

"I damn sure am."

And he did. Whether they liked it or not, three of his best men were flown to Canada on a private jet that very afternoon. They were fully equipped with high capacity magazine assault rifles, powerful hand guns, and all the gear they need to spend a few days in the wilderness. They were met by three men who were survival experts in the wilderness. They were especially familiar with that part of Canada.

They were given photos of Larry Jameson, and were instructed to take him alive. They were told he was a fugitive who scammed the corporation, and that he had knowledge critical to the development of a new gun. That made it a good reason to take him alive.

None of the six men who set out after Larry late that afternoon, had any reason to doubt what they were told. Not when they were paid as much as they were getting for this job. Add to that the fact that he was attempting to hide from corporate officials. he had to be guilty of something.

All that meant, in the final analysis, the secrets he had in his head were so valuable that if all else failed, it would be necessary to kill him.

None of the six men wanted to resort to a killing, so they decided to detour their trip into the wilds. They went, instead, to his homestead. In the hope they could draw him out, they decided to burn his meager homestead to the ground.

It would have worked with most people, but Larry wasn't most people. Once the fires were started, he knew he couldn't do anything about them. He initially was too far away anyway. He quickly closed the gap between where he was and what was once his home. He quickly evaluated the situation.

None of the six men after him had been fully informed about him, so the defenses they organized for waiting for him were actually fairly sloppy. That gave Larry the openings he needed to reverse the situation. Before they even realized there was anyone else around, Larry had four of them subdued. As he took out each of them, he tied and gagged them, then hid them in the thick brush.

The fifth man did put up somewhat of a fight, but his fighting skills didn't come up to Larry's. He was the only one at that point that required that he be knocked out.

The sixth man was simple. Larry just got behind him, stuck a gun in his back, and told him to sit down. The man did. Larry tied him, then told the man what the situation was.

"I'm going to leave you tied the way you are. It's just plastic zip ties holding you, so you will eventually get free. Your five buddies are now tied and tucked away in various niches around here. They can't make much noise, so you'll have to search them out. I'm going to steal your SUV, so after you find everyone, you'll all have to walk to town. When you get there, I will be long gone. If you come after me again, you'll have to find me deep in the woods. The thing is, while you're there I will find you first. When I do, I will kill you and bury you where you fall."

He left it at that, got in the SUV and drove away.

Chapter 31

No one in the Track And Trail club house knew what Carson Chambers had done, or what Derrick's involvement with his activities were, but every one there knew something was wrong. Ideas were floated from person to person and group to group.

Then a new person joined them. She was a normal part of the group, because she was the wife of one of the so-called guides. She'd only returned the previous evening after visiting her mother in another state. Now, this morning, she was back with all her friends at Track And Trail, most of whom were spouses of employees there. Other people enjoying the flow of gossip were a few off-duty employees and several guests of the resort.

After listening for a while about the mysterious, now always referred to as the Amazon Woman, she couldn't help but speak up. She was especially amused by the gross exaggerations about the mystery women. She went to school with Wanda, and still knew and liked her. She was at the shooting exhibition Wanda put on, and like everyone else she was impressed, but still didn't know what the fuss was about.

"I have to tell you all," she said to the group she was sitting with, "that you are making a big deal out of nothing. The woman is Wanda Thomas. She's married to Roy Thomas. Yes, she's good with a rifle and she knows how to defend herself. She's also very pretty, but she's not any goddess. So I certainly don't understand why everyone's making such a big deal out of her."

"Don't you know?" someone asked her, "That Carson Chambers is looking for her. He wants her really bad. He's been searching for her. Someone should tell him who she is."

Someone did. He called Derrick immediately. "Why the hell didn't you know who she was. She's local. You should have known. She's part of those goddamn Thomas's." He paused, breathing heavily. "Since it is so damn obvious that you can't do anything right when left on your own, I'm going to be on a plane very shortly. My people will be there before I get there. I expect you to lead them to that place where those Thomases live. They'll surround it until I arrive. I will then direct them in the capture of my woman, who we now know is Wanda Thomas. We'll just kill all the rest of them."

"You'll end up in jail if you do that."

"No, I won't. Not if I spread enough money around. That'll be your job. I'll supply it, you'll spread it. You got that?"

"I do, but I don't believe it will work."

"Maybe not, Derrick. But it won't be that big a deal if it doesn't. I can always find someone else for a fall guy. It'll be best you remember that."

Derrick hung up having no doubts about who that fall guy would be. He was it, and as cowardly as he'd always been with Carson Chambers, this was too much. He decided that no matter what else happened, he wasn't going to take the fall for that man.

It didn't take a lot of thought about the matter. He would have to do something to stop Carson, or one way or the other, he would be the one in jail. Bribes wouldn't work this time. Like the Thomas family, there was no way sheriff Dale Magee would take a bribe. The man was just too honest, and like so many crazies in that part of the world, he didn't care that much about money. To start covering himself, he did the last thing Carson would have ever suspected him of doing. He called Mack.

"This is who?" Mack said when Derrick identified himself. It was one of those 'why are you calling me' responses.

Derrick repeated his introduction, then said, "I know what I'm going to tell you might sound a little strange, but your life and the lives of your entire family are in danger." He went on with the full story of all that was going on.

When he finished his explanation, Mack asked, "Why are you telling me all this? And why should I believe you?"

"I'm only informing you because I don't want to go to jail. Not because I'm in any way fond of you. In fact, I very much dislike you.

And you should believe me because it sure wouldn't do me any good for me to lie to you about something like this. So get ready for those guys. They are coming."

Mack called Dale first. He put together a small team of deputies and they immediately set out for Mack's.

Mack then called Roy. He then told him what he knew, and asked him to call the rest of the family and tell them they should meet right away at Ben's. Then he went out into the back yard to get Lisa. She was picking vegetables in their kitchen garden for supper.

She didn't notice him, so he moved behind her and wrapped his arms around her. He kissed her on the neck.

"Umm," she said. "I like that."

"Me too. I wanted to do it while I could."

"You can do that, or whatever, to me anytime you want."

"I know, Lisa, but right now we have some big trouble coming."

"No! What is it now?"

Mack explained the situation as they walked to Ben's. As they reached his house, Mack watched Roy and Wanda go in with someone he didn't know. That sent him wondering what else could possibly be happening that they now had a stranger visiting. when there were so many other things going on.

Roy saw the look on his and Lisa's face when they came in, so he answered their questions before they could ask them.

"This is Larry Jameson," Roy said. "He's the man who found Jeffrey Carro's body in his pasture."

Mack shook Larry's hand, then asked, "What brings you to Minnesota?"

"Roy invited me. I wasn't planning on coming here, but when that billionaire bastard had me burned out, I thought it would be a good move. At least for now."

Before they could talk more about it, Dale and the deputies arrived. Dale and the Thomas family gathered around the dining table of Ben's, and the deputies sat in chairs close to the table.

As they sat down, Larry was unsure what to do. Seeing that, Sue pulled the chair next to her out a ways and motioned for him to sit down. As he did, their eyes met. His stomach did a flip flop. She smiled. Wanda noticed the exchange between them. She hoped it would be a good thing for Sue. Even if it was only for a little while.

The talk began then, about the best way to defend themselves, and the farm/ranch that was home to the family.

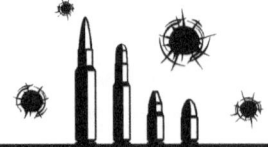

Chapter 32

Derrick James worked himself into a bundle of nerves so tight he was having difficult breathing. What the hell was he going to do with Carson when he got there. He couldn't, no matter how much he hated him, just let him and his men go into the trap he was sure was waiting tor them. Mack wasn't about to ignore his advice. The Thomases, he knew, would be more than ready for Carson and the men already there, waiting for him to arrive.

He knew he was in real trouble. If he let Carson go ahead with his plans, it could only lead to failure. For both of the men. Billionaires or not, there was no good way out of it. Finally, Derrick knew that it no longer mattered what the repercussions might be, he would have to tell Carson the truth. He couldn't let him try to attack the Thomases.

The reaction when he told him after he arrived at the resort was exactly what he expected, with some lethal threats thrown in. "You are now a dead man," Carson screamed. "You might think you're safe, that I won't have you killed, but you are wrong. You are so *definitely dead* wrong."

"I'm really sorry that I had to do what I did, but you didn't give me any choice. If I would have let you go ahead, you would have framed me for the killings."

"Damn right I would have. I still will. I'll be staying here for a few days, along with my people. When things settle down, we'll take those Thomases down. Any problems after, they'll be on you. I can do it easy too. Because by then I will have spread enough money around this county, so that not one soul will be on your side."

Derrick knew he was right. He also knew that there was little he could do about it. Nothing short of killing the man would stop him. If only someone would come along and do it. What a great day it would be with Carson Chambers dead.

He was sitting at his desk. He put his elbows on it, then rested his head in his hands. He stared down, continuing to wish for someone to come and kill the man in the room with him. The man who he hated so much. He knew though, that he was only dreaming. No one was going to save him. There wouldn't even be anyone to help him in any way. One way or the other, everyone was afraid of him and his money.

And that's what it was all about, Just money. But he had money. Only a billion dollars, but that was enough to buy a lot. Probably could buy some good defense attorneys with a lot less than that. Maybe then, there was some help for him. Maybe he could even help himself.

As he stared down at his desk, he thought about what was in his desk drawer. One beautiful, high caliber hand gun. Made by Carson's company. It was just waiting to be used. At least for some threats of his own. He opened the drawer and took out the gun. He looked at the angry, still pacing Carson. Then pointed the gun at him.

"What do you think about this?" he asked loudly.

"Not a damn thing," Carson snarled. "So put the damn thing away before you hurt yourself."

"I'm not going to hurt myself," he answered, smiling now. "The gun is pointed at you."

"If you don't put it away, I will take it away from you."

"I don't think so. Not today."

For the first time, Carson realized he was a serious situation. He knew he had to do something to get Derrick to put the gun away. He moved toward his desk.

At the same time Carson made the move that Derrick considered was threatening, he noticed the fear starting to creep onto Carson's face. It was something he was more than happy to see. It gave him courage. He felt strong now, so he decided to shoot Carson just enough to stop him from coming any closer.

The big problem was the fact that Derrick's mind was no longer functioning normally. In fact, it was barely functioning at all. The confrontation with Carson was now a game. None of this was real to him. All he could think of is keeping him scared.

That wasn't proving to be enough. Carson kept moving toward his desk to take away the gun. So he decided that maybe the best thing to do was shoot him just a little bit. Which he did. And it only made a little hole in his forehead. But it blew away the entire back of Carson's head.

Derrick's secretary rushed into the office when she heard the shot. She fainted when she saw Carson on the floor. The second person into the office called 911. The person who answered that call, called The sheriff's office. They called Dale. He was stunned by what they told him.

He knew that he had to do something right now. But if he wasn't careful about the way he moved, the hired guns around him could easily start shooting. He borrowed a white teeshirt from one of his deputies, tied it to a short stick he found close by on the ground, and moved out from his protected spot waving his new white flag.

"Your boss is dead," he said, loud enough to be heard quite a ways away. "So you might as well hang it up. Get the hell out of here now, and I won't come after you."

It took a while before anyone responded to him. When someone did, it was only a voice coming out of some kind of cover somewhere close. "How do we know you're telling the truth?"

"You don't. But if we all continue waiting this out, every one of you will end up dead or in jail. There are way more of us here than you think, and the Amazon lady is one of them. If you haven't heard, she doesn't miss. I'm guessing that she alone will be killing half of you. At least."

He didn't get another answer, but soon there was a shuffling of bodies. Then, other than some late birds chirping, and a fair amount of insect hum, it grew very quiet.

Since he was already exposed, Dale was the one to look around. The attackers were gone. It was a jubilant bunch that gathered around Dale when he announced that they left.

Mack was the first to ask about Carson Chambers. "You told them he is dead. Is he? If so, how?"

"I don't have the details. I'll let you know as soon as I can, but now I have to check it out."

It felt strange for Mack and Lisa to not be going with him when he left. Part of them still felt like deputies. Yet, at the same time, it somehow felt good to be able to skip attending another bloody crime scene.

The Thomases decided then that it was late enough in the day to eat. But since they'd had so much excitement and none of them felt like doing any kind of work, they once again went to the Mystic Curve Inn. The first thing they talked about when they got there was Larry.

It surprised him that they were all so interested in him and what his plans were. Roy was the first to ask, "You are planning to stay with us, aren't you?"

"I don't know. I don't want to be a burden to anyone, and I don't want to be in the way. I think, if I stayed with you and Wanda for very long, I would surely get in the way."

Sue, who was surprising herself, was feeling somewhat attracted to him. She wasn't sure why, other than he was tall and handsome, seemed to be strong and humble at the same time, and came across as an altogether nice guy. Still, she didn't say anything about where he should stay right away.

"Well," Roy offered, "at least stay for the next few days. That won't at all burden us, nor will you get in the way or interfere with our lives."

"I guess I can stay for a couple of days. Maybe by then, things will have settled down enough so I can go back home."

Sue decided then, that it would be interesting if he could be convinced to stay longer. So she made the offer that she'd been running through her mind. "You know, you guys, I live alone and I do have a spare room. It isn't all that large, but it does have a queen size bed, it's private, and it might work for Larry. If, that is, he wants to stay in it?"

Larry was at a loss for words, so all he could do was stare at her. What was such a good looking woman doing, trusting him to stay with her. Wanda again picked up on what he was thinking.

She cleared her throat to get his attention, looked him in the eye, and said, "She trusts you because Roy and I do. She feels safe because she has family close. No one with even half a brain would do her any kind of harm with all of us around. And being a single woman, why wouldn't she want a handsome man like you around for company."

Larry blushed heavily from her comments, shook his head in wonder over this strange bunch sitting with him, and finally said, "Miss Sue, I'll take it as an honor to stay in that extra room of yours. And rest assured, I will always treat you with the utmost respect."

It was settled then. Larry would stay at Sue's. He had agreed to it too, without any further consideration of how long he would stay.

They spent a quiet moment then, enjoying the peaceful feeling that can only happen at the gathering of a family who deeply cared each other. The feeling was short lived, however.

About twenty people, mostly males who were employees of Track And Trail, drove into the parking lot of the bar in various vehicles. The people piled out and stomped inside. They weren't drunk yet, but all of them had been drinking heavily. The first through the door spotted the Thomases right away.

"Well lookee here," one of the men said, "if it isn't the trouble making bunch who think they know it all."

"By damn," another man said, "it sure as hell is. After all the trouble today, brought on mostly by them, I think maybe it's time to kick some ass."

Wanda, who was at this paint totally fed up with men who thought they were macho enough to beat the hell out of anyone, left her chair and faced the men.

"Lisa, Sue, and Theresa, I want you to stand up." She looked around the table. "For now, I want the rest of you to stay where you are."

She stepped away from the table and motioned for the other three women to stand next to her. When they did, she pointed at the two men who had mouthed off, lifted both hands, and waved her fingers as an invitation for them to come to her and start something. The other three soon joined her, motioning for the entire group from the resort to try something with them. No one made a move toward them.

"Well," Wanda said, "what's the matter. All you hotshot men afraid to take on four little women. I ain't no Amazon goddess. I'm just a good man's wife who's well fed up with this kind of crap. So come and get me, Tonight, I am more than ready to kick some ass."

Lisa joined in then. "I just want all you guys to know. You started this, but we will finish it. I for sure do not intend on taking any prisoners.

When I am done, each and everyone of you will be in the hospital. The pain you have then, will last you a long time."

She smile, and again waved her fingers. Quiet filled the bar. No one in the crowd knew what to do. A fight with the men would have been simple enough, but what do you do with four crazy women.

In the end the answer was nothing. The new crowd dispersed and they managed to get through the night without so much as even a small threat or a cross word.

For about an hour before they went home, music played on the jukebox. Mack and Roy changed partners a couple of times, but Ben and Theresa danced together the whole time. What was noticed though, was the fact that so did Sue and Larry.

Chapter 33

Shanty Lucas, Carson Chambers daughter, didn't go to her father's funeral. She had zero desire to go through all the phony pageantry that was going to be his service. Instead, she sat up in the cot in the surgery room, waiting as patiently as she could for the doctor.

He arrived with an empty smile that he hoped would be reassuring to her. It wasn't. "Well," he said, "what do you think? Are you ready to see how the healing has progressed?"

"Not at all," she answered, "But let's get it done." Inside, she knew that she wasn't going to like what she was going to see when the bandages came off her face. Her husband went way beyond a typical beating when he attacked her, and she knew that at least some of the scars were going to be permanent. Plastic surgery or not.

The doctor worked obscenely slow as he peeled away the bandages. It didn't help. The scars were still there when the bandages were gone. She hated her dead husband for what he did to her, but she blamed her dead father for it happening. He's the one who didn't give a damn when her husband knew exactly what he was doing to her.

She knew too, that the final truth was the fact that it was her own fault. She'd never done anything to stop him. She loved the money too much. All those years she whored for her father, just for the money. But it was all hers now. Her mother was the only one other than her to get any of the money or investments, and she got enough to live an easy life, for however long she lived.

But Shanty had more than just money. She had the power to do about anything she wanted to do, as long as it was legal. And what she wanted to do was a lot of things that would piss off her father, if he was alive to get pissed off. Number one on that list was the Thomas family. Rather than do anything to hurt them, she was now going to check them out, and do whatever she could to make their life better.

She was also very curious about the private wildlife refuge that they were involved with. It was something she didn't know much about, but thought it might be interesting to get involved in it. So, from now on, she was going to be busy doing things her father would have hated.

She knew that the best place to start with those projects was with what was now essentially her business, Life's Protection Corporation. Most of what the company did was okay with her. She considered hunting to be a legitimate sport, and thought target shooting was fun. But she hated assault rifles, and believed they should be banned from American society. She knew she couldn't do that on her own, but she also knew that she could stop that division of the company. At least her company could stop making the evil things. So she found jobs for everyone who worked in that part of gun making, and shut it down. She knew it would only be a matter of time before those assets could be put to work again, manufacturing something useful.

After that, she thought about all the deserving organizations, people, and projects she could contribute to. But so far, there was little she knew how to do. She'd essentially wasted her life doing nothing but spending her father's money on things she rarely cared anything about, traveling to places she paid little attention to while she was there, and having a lot of sex. She hated what she was forced to do with her father. What happened with her husband had on rare occasions been almost pleasurable. And what bothered her was the fact that only the men who were one-time lovers had ever given her any real satisfaction. So she was lost when it came to knowing what to do or who to help next.

She tried to get advice from people who worked for her, but all any of the could tell her were the best ways to keep all her money. The one thing she most wanted to help, to do something to stop the constant destruction of, was the environment. The trouble was, there was almost no one in her world who had even the smallest bit of interest in it or concern for it. The few that did care, were afraid to talk about it, for fear of the repercussions that might result from discussing something that might cost some billionaire more than a dime.

The other problem was, no matter where she looked, no matter who or what she sought out for help in deciding where she should start, the answer was, "Give me money."

She had no abjection to donating money. Her concern was the fact she never knew who was legitimately deserving and who wasn't. So she took herself out of the public eye, and spent a considerable amount of time doing research on all of the things which now held her interest.

Chapter 34

It was relatively quiet around the Refuge Rescue Agency for the next couple of weeks. Rather than be concerned for the business, it was a welcome relief for everyone involved. Mack and Lisa spent a good deal of the time working with lawyers, who were putting together lawsuits against all the various hunting resort/lodges along the St Catherine River.

They had gathered more than sufficient evidence of their polluting to sue everyone of them on behalf of the wildlife refuge. Mack was the one who spent the most time with the lawyers, because he was the chairman of the board that managed the refuge. Lisa spent a lot of time in those meetings, because she had helped Mack gather so much of the evidence to be used against those companies.

Wanda and Roy used the time to drive to his ranch in Texas. The purpose of the trip was to sell the ranch. It was an easy task. They sold it to the couple who had managed it for them for many years. The terms Roy gave them were more than fair, and designed so that the couple would have no trouble making payments on it.

After everything was settled with the ranch, they decided to make the trip home a site seeing tour. They drove west through New Mexico, then spent a night in Tucson. From there they went to the Grand Canyon. It proved to be a hassle, rather than a fun visit to the wondrous place it once was. There were so many people visiting that it was difficult at best to even get near any of the beautiful vistas they'd visited in the past. So they gave up on it early. From there they drove up through Monument Valley, stopping at all of the national parks. From there, the trip home felt like a long one.

Even so, they appreciated the trip and all the beautiful scenery along the way. But rather than it being the relaxing time they hoped for, they arrived even more tired than they were when they started the trip.

For Ben and Theresa, life went on as normal. His garden crops were producing heavily, as they always did, and that was more than enough to keep them busy. Theresa's time, when she wasn't working directly with Ben, was largely spent canning and freezing. Since she was putting up food for all of them, she had little time to waste.

Sue filled in her time working with Mack and sometimes the lawyers, doing research for the detective agency, and showing Larry around the area.

They somehow knew the day they met, that there would be something between them. That something quickly grew from a simple friendship to some strong romantic feelings. At first, they did their best to avoid any physical contact. No matter what feelings they might have, they were both very aware of Larry's leaving sometime in the future and returning to Canada.

But fate doesn't always cooperate. Not even with the best of intentions. It took charge of them one evening when they went out for a hamburger and fries. After they ate, someone played a dollar's worth of country love songs on the jukebox. They danced, and before the end of the second song, they were holding each other tight.

The ride home from the bar was silent. when they went into the house, Sue planned to quickly go into her office and pretend to work. Before she could, however, he touched her shoulder. She turned to face him and he kissed her. It was too late for them then.

She took his hand and led him to her bedroom. He spent the night there. After that, the spare bedroom sat unused. Their affair made them happy, and brought a lot of joy to their lives. It also all too often left them terrified. What would they do, how would they manage it, when the time came for him to go back home.

And it didn't take long for the possibility of that to become more than a possibility. It was early afternoon when Mack got a call he nearly didn't answer.

"May I please speak to a mister Mack Thomas?" the voice on the other end of the line asked when he answered the phone, without first looking at the caller ID.

"I don't know," he said, his voice somewhat grumpy. "who is calling?"

The lady sighed. "I'm just a secretary. I'm calling for MZ Shanty Lucas. She is the CEO of the Life's Protection Corporation. Her father was the founder of the corporation, Carson Chambers. She would very much like to speak to you."

"Why would she want to talk to me. She's rich and famous and I'm very much nobody. So I'm close to hanging up on you. I think this is just another scam."

"I assure you mister Mack Thomas, this is not a scam. MZ Lucas is interested in the many environmental issues we are all facing, and she would like to have the opportunity to discuss them with you."

"Again, why me. There are many thousands, of people better qualified to talk to than me."

"Maybe, but she prefers to speak with you. Will you talk to her?"

"I'm still not at all sure about this call, but what the hell, I'll listen to her for a short time, if it is in fact actually her. The first hint of wanting money though, and I will be hanging up."

"I'll connect you now."

Mack heard some clicks and hums, then a new voice on the phone. "Are you still there, mister Thomas?" the lady asked.

"I am. What can I do for you?"

"I'm so glad I finally reached you. You have some people there who are very good at filtering your calls."

"With the number of crank calls we get, we have to be good at it. So now that you've got me, tell me what it is you want. I don't mean to be nasty, but I don't have a lot of time for trivial bullshit."

"Given your reputation," Shanty said, "I wouldn't expect anything else."

"That's good. So can we get on with this?"

Mack's voice continued to have a growl in it, and she sensed it in the tone of his voice. "I do apologize for taking so much of your time. With the many things I wish to speak with you about, I would like to meet you and your wife, Lisa, in person. It's the only way we can adequately cover everything I very much want to go over with you."

"That will be difficult, to say the least. From what I know, you live somewhere outside of New York City. That's a long way from Minnesota."

"Not if I fly you here in my private jet, and put you up in a luxury suite in the hotel of your choice. Meals, drinks, and anything else you might want will also be included."

"I don't think so, Miss Lucas. I don't have even the slightest interest in spending time in a hotel in a big city, no matter how fancy."

"Are you sure about that. I guaranty it will be to your benefit."

"I still don't think so. I'll tell you what though, since you're so interested in getting together with me to talk, and are trying to make it seem important, why don't you come here. If our talk gets too late in the day, one of us can put you up for the night. Or you can stay at a local motel. I think our airport will be able to handle your plane, if it isn't too big."

She laughed. "And what kind of accommodations do you have for guests?"

"Each of us has a spare bedroom. Size on average, about ten by twelve feet. Queen bed in all but one house. There's a double bed in that one. All of the houses are ordinary middle class ramblers. Nothing fancy."

She laughed again. "Doesn't sound at all like something I'm used to."

"I didn't think so. It would be my guess then, that we can forget about making contact with each other. It's ben interesting talking to you, but I'm going back to work now."

"Just wait a minute now. I didn't say I wouldn't come. I just don't want to impose on any of you. I will rent an RV, and have it waiting for me when my plane lands. Now all you have to do is tell me where, when, and what time."

They worked out the details, and finally hung up the phones. Mack still wasn't sure about the call, and figured that even if it really was who she said she was, she would never show up. Billionaires just didn't spend their time with ordinary people.

He told everyone about the call, and requested they be there at the scheduled time and place anyway. Then they waited.

Chapter 35

It was a surprise to all of them when the forty-six foot, custom RV pulled it the driveway and parked near Ben and Theresa's. Mack and Lisa were waiting for Shanty, when she followed what they took as her body guard, out of the RV.

She was grossly over-dressed for the people and place she was visiting. Her outfit was both beautiful and sexy. It managed to accent all of her feminine attributes without in any way making her look cheap. Her appearance shocked all of them though. The last thing they'd expected to see were the deep scars on her once beautiful face.

Knowing what there reaction would be, and wanting to immediately clear the air about it, she bluntly explained the scars. She did, however, neglect to tell them how her father caused the incident. That part she felt, was best left private.

She looked at Mack, who she recognized from pictures of him she found while researching him, when she spoke. "The scars are from a beating I got from my husband just before my father shot and killed him. I'm telling you this now, so none of you have to wonder about it. I want all of us to be able to concentrate on the many things I want to discuss with you, and not think about my scars." She smiled.

Mack answered quickly and as honestly as he could. "We'll do our best to do that."

He took a moment then, to introduce everyone there. When he got to Sue, he did not explain how she was now part of the family. With Larry, Shanty raised her eyebrows when Mack explained who he was.

When he completed the introductions, he said, "And now it's time for breakfast."

He took her elbow, then motioned for the man with her that he was welcome inside too, and led her into Ben and Theresa's dining room. They left the seat at the head of the table empty for Ben, and the seat to his right for Theresa. Mack sat down next to Shanty, then motioned for the man with her to sit on the other side of her.

Extra chairs were added to the table setting, making it somewhat crowded, but Mack was determined to have everyone at this table. He wanted them all, even Larry, in on this conversation.

As soon as Ben and Theresa brought in the first platters of food, Mack introduced Ben and Theresa. They both responded, "Nice to meet you," and went back to the kitchen for more food.

Shanty was overwhelmed by the loaded platters. First was the meat. Thick sliced bacon, fried a perfect crispy brown. Breakfast sausage in links and patties. Smoked sausage in long, fat links. And finally, generous slices of home smoked ham.

Eggs came scrambled, over easy, and made into omelets. Next to them was buttered toast and fresh baked biscuits. A platter was filled with half hash brown and half home fried potatoes.

A small plate of home grown sliced tomatoes was next to a large bowl of cantaloupe pieces, fresh picked the previous day. Finally, it was all rounded off with a bowl of fresh picked raspberries, with whipped cream on the side.

As the food was passed around, Shanty found herself staring with unbelieving awe at the amount of food being piled on plates. Mack, Ben, and Roy were eating enough food for two or three men each. Yet, none of them had an ounce of extra fat on them.

Lisa though, shocked her the most. Here was this petite little woman putting down a plate of food that would defeat most big men. More astounding than that, she managed to do it in a rather dainty fashion.

All that was followed by a most pleasant surprise. The food. As good as it all looked, she was skeptical of all of it when she put very moderate portions of only a few things on her plate. That changed big time when she tasted it.

For a person who had eaten in expensive restaurants all over the world, she still hadn't ever sampled flavors like she was now. After the first two bites, she looked around the room, a huge smile on her face.

"Where," she asked loud enough for everyone to hear, "did you manage to find food this good. Someone must have been shopping for days to find it." She looked at Theresa. "And where did you learn to cook like this. Not many chefs anywhere could match this."

Theresa answered her. "To start with, I only helped with the cooking. Ben does most of it. And one of the reasons we are good with breakfast is because we cook it for the family every morning."

"You're kidding? Everyday?"

"They do," Mack answered. "It kind of started with dad and I when I first came back home after riding rodeo. It just somehow grew into a kind of tradition that we do every day."

"It's something," Lisa added, "that now, if it stopped, would leave a big hole in our lives."

"I would imagine it would," Shanty said. "But you can't possibly eat this good every day. It must be difficult to consistently find food this good."

"Actually," Theresa explained, "it is easy to find. It does take some effort though, to grow and raise it. We pasture about five hundred laying hens. I used to sell most of the eggs, but now what we don't eat go to the local food self."

"That's only one thing. There's a ton of food on this table."

"We all have a kitchen garden," Theresa said, "and what vegetables we don't grow there, we get from Ben. He raises about forty acres of vegetables for the farmer's market every year. I can and freeze too. I usually manage to put up enough to get us all through the winter. As far as the meat goes, we raise our own pigs. We have them processed locally. That's why the flavor is what it is. We treat them and feed them right."

Shanty was surprised by all of that. When she'd checked on Mack, it started with his record as a sheriff's deputy. That led to Lisa, so she was checked too. She'd also looked into his involvement with the wildlife refuge, but not in as much depth as law enforcement.

She did know though, that he was deeply interested in environmental problems, and had used that interest to get his attention. She was sure too, that he was well versed enough on the subject to be able to answer some of her questions.

When she started to ask them though, he put her off. "What I'd like to do," he told her, "is take you on a walk through at least a part of the refuge, so you can see first hand what's going on there. The problems we are having, and the cause of the problems we're having, might surprise you. Especially since one of your companies is responsible for a large portion of it."

"If that's the case, yes, I am most definitely interested in seeing it."

When they finished eating, Mack asked Shanty if she had a change of clothes with her.

"Sure," she said, "but what's wrong with what I have on?"

"They won't work for hiking. You't get anywhere down the trail with the shoes you're wearing. High heels just don't make on the soft ground."

"Oh, well, I thought we'd be riding in something."

"Sorry, but we don't allow any kind of vehicles in the refuge. Horses either. The place is first for the wildlife there. Animals, plants, and even the bugs, as long as it's all native. So walking is the only way you can see it. We can skip it though. It's probably not that important anyway."

"It is to me, Mack. Maybe I could get a ride to town, where I can buy the right clothes."

Wanda spoke up. "That's not necessary. You and I are close enough in size, so you should be able to wear something of mine."

"Are you sure? I don't want to impose on you."

"You won't be imposing at all. I really want you to see the refuge. It's something Mack has worked awful hard, for a long time, to save. If the rich people in this part of the world had their way, it would have been gone a long time ago."

"So, because I'm rich, you want to be sure I see it?"

"That's exactly right. I'm not trying to offend you. But I have to tell you, people who have the kind of money, or even close to the kind money you have, tend to live in a very different world than what we do. And all of you are way out of touch with reality. You think money is what makes the world go round. The truth is, money is destroying it."

Shanty did the unexpected then. She smiled. "I know, Wanda. That's why I came here. To learn reality, and if there was something i could do with all the money I have to be able to make it better. And I don't mean to offend you either, but you are part of the reason I decided to make the trip here. This is not something I would normally do."

"How could I possibly be someone you wanted to see. Mack, Roy, and Ben can answer your questions better than I can. Likely as not, Theresa, Lisa, and Sue can answer them as well as me, if not better."

"I don't doubt that." Shanty tried not too, but she laughed. "But you see, Wanda, you are the only one who is a goddess. If you could have seen my father lust over you the way he did, you would be curious about you too."

"Well, it's got to be obvious to you now, that I am anything but a goddess. I'm just a real ordinary woman lucky enough to be married to one of the greatest guys anyone could ever find."

"No, Wanda, you are not ordinary." Shanty looked up at the ceiling, as if to find the right words. "In the short time I've been here, I've come to the conclusion that none of you are ordinary. So let's get a move on, and get me into the right clothes for whatever Mack has in mind for me."

They got Shanty ready and left for the refuge. They weren't far into it before Shanty wondered what the fuss was about. She expected to see woods with giant ancient trees, and all there is is shrubs and new growth trees. It was a decent year for rain, so the grasslands were still a lush green, and enough wild flowers to add a splash go color here and there. But to her, it looked rather barren.

When she asked Mack about the trees, he explained about the fire and how to the average person it didn't look like the refuge was actually recovering much. When he finished explaining how the recovery really was happening, he told her about the existing problems and how serious they were.

"In fact," he told her, "the board who supervises his refuge is in the process of putting together a series of lawsuits against your company, Track And Trail, to stop their pollution of the river supplying much of the water needed for the many wetlands here. There are others polluting too, who will be sued, but your company is the worst."

"I know a little bit about that place. That's where they accidentally shot that man and then tried to get rid of the body in Canada."

"It is, and Larry's the man who found the body."

"Really? But why is he here?"

"Roy and Wanda went to Canada to talk to him about it. While they were there your father tried to kidnap Wanda and kill Roy and

Larry. Then they burned him out. So on Roy's invite he came here. He and Sue got hooked up, so he's staying on for a while."

"I sort of get all that, but why were Roy and Wanda up there to talk to him?"

"We were investigating the shooting for a client."

When they reached the river, and even she could see the pollution problems caused by the resort/lodges, it visibly upset her.

"I sure can see why you are suing all those people," she said. "This is terrible." She quietly watched the water for a while, then turned to Mack again. "If you don't mind, Mack, I would very much appreciate it if you would take me to Track And Trail. I want to see for myself what they're doing."

She showed no interest in the clubhouse or talking to any of the management of the place. What she most wanted to see were the various animals. She found the conditions they lived in to be what she called, an abomination. By the time she finished the tour, she was beyond angry.

"I don't know what to tell you exactly, Mack. But I'm asking you for a favor. Will you please give me a couple of weeks before you file those lawsuits. I might have a better way of dealing with this."

The rest of the day was primarily spent sitting in a circle on the ground in Ben's back yard, on the small patch of grass he called his lawn. They talked about all the various things Shanty was interested in, along with many of the concerns.

She was especially sympathetic to Larry's difficulties in Canada, and promised to see what she could do to help. Sue wanted to tell her not to, but knew that any comments like that would only come across as selfish on her part.

Dale joined them late in the afternoon. He brought his wife, Kathy along. For the first time in a while, she was taking a break from her singing tours, so they were all glad to see her. She even sang a few songs for them, which proved to be a special treat for Shanty. She was already a big fan of Kathy's music.

Ben and Theresa put together a supper that they could eat off paper plates with a minimum mess, and again, Shanty was impressed with the food.

They stayed together until late, and even then they hated to break it up. Shanty had tears in her eyes when she said goodnight to all of them. She was leaving early in the morning, so it was goodby too. At least for a while.

Mack and Lisa were the last to walk to their house after she boarded the RV. Lisa held his hand especially tight as they did.

She kissed him when they got in the house. "I don't ever want to have to tell you goodbye," she told Mack. "Not even if it's only two days, and not for any reason."

"I love you too," he said.

Epilogue

errick James never made it to trial. He was found mentally incompetent after he put the bullet in the head of Carson Chambers. No one hated him for the crime. Certainly not Shanty Lucas. She felt nothing toward him. Not even any sympathy. A few others did. Just as a lot of people secretly thanked him. Carson Chambers was anything but a popular man.

*****

Few people paid attention to the storm when it hit. That was because there were few people in that part of the mountains. The rain, when it came, came down in sheets so thick visibility went to near zero. As it rushed down the highway it increased to the point it was moving rocks several feet in diameter. When the wall of water reached the canyon and rushed over the side, it carried the rocks with it.

As they fell, they slammed into the sides of the canyon, knocking even more rocks loose. Soon, the deluge of rocks and water took one side of the canyon wall down with it. As it did, it buried a SUV, lying on its roof, with the bodies of five well burned dead in it, with a couple hundred tons of rocks and dirt. The material was deep enough, so that it would be unlikely that anyone would ever know the SUV was there. Not for a few hundred years anyway.

*****

Sue stayed close to Larry after Shanty left. The signs were small, but it seemed to be evident to her that Larry was going through some kind of change.

He was still attentive to her needs, and not a night went by without him making love to her before they slept. Even so, her life she now loved was slipping away.

Deep down she knew. She'd known all along. What they had was temporary. He was going home to Canada. It was just a matter of time. She knew too, that he would ask her to come with him. But she knew her answer was no.

She had no wish to leave this family who brought her in and now considered her to be one of them. But that wasn't all of it. She loved the wild places, much like everyone in her adopted family. But she wasn't prepared for a subsistence kind of life. She needed all the things and activity her life now provided.

So all she could do was love and share what she had with Larry while she still had him. However long that might be.

*****

Dale had enough evidence from his own investigation, and from all that Refuge Rescuers had gathered, to arrest the management of Track and Trail for covering up the shooting Jeffry Carro. They were also charged for dumping his body. The men who flew the plane lost their licenses and had to find a different career from flying.

*****

Shanty came through with her promise to do something about Track and Trail. She shut it down. After visiting a couple more of them, she shut them all down for hunting, along with their cruelty to animals. They were turned instead, into educational centers dedicated to teaching intercity children about wildlife and natural places for them to love.

The one in Clayborne County was donated to the refuge, with the hope that the refuge commission would find a way to turn it into a community learning center. One that was dedicated to teaching about the environment and how critical it was to preserve at least part of it. It also added two thousand acres to the refuge.

Along with that. she purchased all of the remaining hunting resort/ lodges, and hired a management company to run them. They were to be used mainly for senior citizens who needed assistance to visit the refuge. In order to do this, she managed to get permission to use various electric vehicles to transport them. Another plus in the deal, was the fact that some of the larger suites in them were converted to assisted living housing for seniors and the disabled.

The final good thing that resulted from shutting down the Track And Trail resorts was the cancelling of the contract with the government to sell the resort company part of the Saguaro National Park. Both of the Republican senators from Arizona, along with the Republican governor, screamed for Shanty's head because of it. She ignored them. The contract for the purchase was non-binding, so there was nothing they could do about it.

*****

It didn't take Refuge Rescuers long to gather the evidence of years of graft against five of the commissioners. It was turned over to the county attorney, and he filed charges against them. They never went to trial though. They rather chose to admit to their guilt in order to plea bargain their sentences down to half.

The next election, the seats were filled by three independents and two Democrats. All five were liberals. All of them pleaded with Mack and Lisa to return to the sheriff's department. They were sorely missed. They turned down the offer.

*****

Mack was surprised the morning the UPS truck arrived and delivered a fairly thick brown envelope that he was required to sign for. He dreaded opening it, sure that something from some big law firm in New York had to be some terrible news.

It wasn't. It was the papers describing a trust fund created for Refuge Rescuers. It was only to be used for deserving clients who needed but could not afford their services. The amount of money was beyond what they could use. But coming from Shanty, that was no surprise. The numbers she lived by were so far removed from everyday life that Mack knew she'd never understand, no matter how he explained it.

So he didn't try. Instead he excepted it and gave everyone but himself and Lisa a raise. He knew they could get by without it, but felt that they could do a better job if they didn't have any money concerns.

****

Shanty called him before she attempted the next thing she wanted to do. Her question was about something he hadn't thought of.

"What do you think," she asked, "about putting together a crew, with whatever equipment to clean up the river? Upstream of it and inside the refuge. I'll cover the costs, if you'll put the thing together?"

"It sounds great. I'll start working on it right away. It'll be slow going though. we will need to do it all by hand. If we use machines of any size at all, it could do more damage than the pollution."

"That's fine. All I care, is that it gets done."

"We'll do it then."

"Good. While I have you on the phone, I have two other things to tell you. Both good news I hope. First off, I want you to tell Larry that I've had his entire homestead rebuilt. A little better I think, then what it was. And last, I want to take a day soon, and have breakfast with you and your family. And maybe make a day of it. I never did explore enough of that refuge of yours to satisfy me."

"I think," Mack answered her, "I would love to have you spend a day with us. Just let me know when, an I'll make sure everyone schedules that day off."

They talked further before they ended the call. By then, Mack had a heavy knot in his gut. He knew that Larry would be happy to hear about his home, but he dreaded what it would do Sue.

He knew Larry would be leaving now, and he knew that his going would break Sue's heart. He couldn't help but wish someone could do something to ease her pain. He should have thought of their very own wonder woman. Wanda.

*****

Sue cried when she heard the news. Larry told her not to worry. He wasn't going to leave her. Not right away. All he was going to do was fly up to Canada and see what was done to his homestead. He would be back in two days.

They made love twice that night. In the morning Larry took a local cab to the airport alone. He said he hated saying goodbye in airports.

Sue waited for the call he promised to make when he got to his homestead. It didn't come. When she called him, his new phone went directly to voice mail. It continued to do so until Sue gave up the evening of the second day he was gone. He wasn't coming back and she knew it.

Wanda was with her when she fully realized it. She held Sue as she broke down, crying so hard she was helpless.

Wanda held her for a while, but knew that short of Larry returning, there was only one way Sue could be comforted at all. She called Roy and told him to come over. She met him at the front door and took him in the kitchen, away from Sue.

"I know that this will sound strange to you," she said, "but let me finish talking and you will understand. Sue is hurting really bad now. And you are the only one who can give her the comfort she needs. You are her best friend, her mentor, and someone she loves every bit as much as she loves Larry. I'm going home now. I want you to stay with her. It's not so crazy as you might think. You trusted me so many times, back when Mack was having those terrible nightmares. Think now, how many times I just held him until they stopped. I trust you to do the same with Sue. You might just hold her hand and be there for her. Or maybe hold her tight. It'll be okay, even if you hold her in bed until she sleeps. And you have to know this too, Roy. I won't like it if it goes further than that. Especially if it's a lot further. But it will be okay. She is what matters right now. All the rest will just have to work itself out."

She left him then. He moved to Sue. He took her hand. She looked at him through the tears in her eyes. A bolt of fear slammed through him when their eyes met.

*****

"Wanda called," Lisa said to Mack. "She left Roy with Sue, to comfort her. What do you think that's about."

"I don't think it's about anything to worry about. Roy is her best friend. He has been since shortly after they met. So it only makes sense that he would be there for her."

"I know, but sometimes things like that can lead to a lot more than just comforting."

"I don't think so. Nothing's going to happen."

"I'm glad you're so sure, Mack. All I know is that if something like that would have happened between me and you back when we were still just friends, I would have done my very best to seduce you."

"No, you would never have done something like that."

"You're right. I wouldn't have done that with anyone else in the world. Except you." She got up, then sat in his lap. "I'm here now," she giggled, "to do that very thing to you."

She twisted around in his lap, then kissed his neck. He moved her head and kissed her lips. She returned it.

"I'll tell you what, Mack. I want to pretend that you are just my best friend and that I need comforting. Can you comfort me for a little while."

Mack thought about it, and decided that if she wanted comforting, he could probably manage to do it all night if that's what it took.

Any and all other problems they or the world had, would still be there in the morning. He was just happy that they'd recently solved so many without the violence that all too often went along with solving them.

Life was good right now, and Lisa was seeing to it that it was getting ever better. The love he felt for her then, temporarily chased away all of the past nightmares.